Lord help her, that first touch of his mouth on hers was like she had touched a live wire. She felt a jolt of electricity shoot through her body. It was as though a part of her had been shocked back to life.

Her heart pounded out of control as Mason began to move his lips over hers with tantalizing slowness. Sweet heat spread through her.

And it felt so good.

Sabrina let herself surrender to the kiss. She let herself surrender to this gorgeous man. Because there was something thrilling about being chased….

But then thoughts filled her brain that jarred her from the moment. Cat and mouse. A game. This wasn't real, just something for Mason to entertain himself with.

Her lust subsiding, Sabrina broke the kiss and pushed him away from her, then quickly stepped past him.

She breathed in and out heavily, catching her breath. Regaining her sanity. Why had she allowed him to kiss her like that? As though he had any rights to her?

"Why did you do that?" she demanded. "And after I told you to leave."

"Are you saying you didn't like it?"

"You can't just go around kissing people! There are laws against that!"

Mason flashed her an easy smile. "If I'm guilty of liking you, then I'll do the time."

Books by Kayla Perrin

Harlequin Kimani Romance

KAYLA PERRIN

has been writing since the age of thirteen and once entertained the idea of becoming a teacher. Instead, she has become a *USA TODAY* and *Essence* bestselling author of dozens of mainstream and romance novels, and has been recognized for her talent, including twice winning Romance Writers of America's Top Ten Favorite Books of the Year Award. She has also won the Career Achievement Award for multicultural romance from *RT Book Reviews*. Kayla lives with her daughter in Ontario, Canada.

Burning
DESIRE

Kayla Perrin

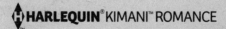

HARLEQUIN® KIMANI™ ROMANCE

This book is dedicated to first responders everywhere.

Thank you for your brave acts of heroism that make a difference in people's lives every day.

Recycling programs
for this product may
not exist in your area.

ISBN-13: 978-0-373-86358-7

BURNING DESIRE

Copyright © 2014 by Kayla Perrin

For questions and comments about the quality of this book please contact us at CustomerService@Harlequin.com.

Printed in U.S.A.

www.Harlequin.com

Dear Reader,

What is it about a uniform that makes a man that much sexier? Whether a police officer, naval captain or firefighter, there's something incredibly sexy about a man in uniform.

Maybe it's the fact that we know the men wearing these uniforms are strong, noble and can save you when your life is in duress. Or maybe it's just because they look good in their attire.

Sabrina Crawford has what many would consider a dream job: she's creating the annual firefighter's calendar. But for her, it's just another job. Having suffered one too many heartbreaks at the hands of a gorgeous man, she's immune to the men she's photographing. Though Mason Foley certainly gets her blood boiling—in more ways than one. Sabrina's determined not to succumb to his charms. Mason is determined to make her his.

Welcome to the world of the Ocean City Fire Department. I'm excited to be writing about firefighters for the first time in a new series for Harlequin Kimani Romance. I hope you enjoy the first book!

Kayla Perrin

Chapter 1

The flames raged out of control, consuming Jodi's Steakhouse, a popular new restaurant in Ocean City's downtown core. The sparks flickered in the night, illuminating the dark sky in a dance that was both magical and menacing.

Mason Foley, captain at Station Two of the Ocean City Fire Department, led the charge, doing what he did best—battling the fire. In many ways, he was like a gladiator stepping into a coliseum, knowing that with each battle it was kill or be killed.

And he would do everything in his power to emerge the victor.

At least there was no one inside the building, something that had been determined from the initial 911 call. And when Mason and his team had first gone into the building, they had used their thermal cameras to determine that indeed, there were no bodies inside. Given that it was nearly four in the morning, it hadn't been likely that they would find anyone in the restaurant, but you could never be too sure.

But despite the early hour, there was chaos around him on the downtown streets. People who were up at this time had converged on the scene to watch the firefighters battle the blaze. Others observed from the windows of the condominium across the street.

While some captains did more overseeing and doling out of responsibilities at a fire scene, Mason believed in getting his hands dirty. After giving his team directions, he and Omar Duncan, a friend as well as a colleague, held a hose on the dying flames licking the inside of the building. Firefighters from the ladder truck had vented the roof, and then proceeded to attack the fire with hoses from the aerial ladder.

An hour and a half later, the fire was out. The battle was won. And most importantly, the men and women of Station Two had kept the fire from spreading to the neighboring restaurants.

Mason's body was filled with adrenaline, and though he should be tired, he didn't feel any exhaustion. He pulled his oxygen mask from his face as he exited the building. He walked to the middle of the street and surveyed the damage. Smoke still billowed into the sky, and the once upscale restaurant was now a burned-out shell.

Tyler, one of his best friends and the engineer in charge of the pump truck, approached him and gave him a pat on the shoulder. "Good job, man."

"You, too."

Tyler followed Mason's line of sight to the burned structure, then faced him again. "I know that look. What are you thinking?"

"Second restaurant fire in a week? Same hour of night? I'm wondering if we've got a serial arsonist on our hands."

"The same thought crossed my mind," Tyler said.

Mason walked back toward the building, passing firefighters who were drinking water and opening their heavy jackets to cool down. He headed straight for the restaurant's back door to see if his hunch was right. Amid the debris he found what he had at the other scene, five days earlier. Signs that the back door had been pried open, as well as a discarded gasoline can in the back alley.

"Great," he uttered, exhaling in aggravation. "Definitely arson."

"You think the M.O.'s the same as the last restaurant?"

Mason turned around to find Tyler standing a few feet behind him. "Gas can in the alley." He pointed. "From the scraping and indentation on the door, you can tell that it's been pried open, probably with a crow bar."

"Exactly like the first time," Tyler commented wryly. "What happened—this guy get food poisoning or something and now he's taking it out on the city?"

The police were already trying to find the person behind the first arson, with no luck thus far. Hopefully, he had made a mistake with this one and left some sort of clue behind. If he had burned himself, he would likely end up at one of the area hospitals or even one outside the city limits.

"We need to track this guy down before he strikes again," Mason said.

"Or her," Tyler corrected.

"Or her," Mason agreed. Two years ago, a female arsonist had started three fires before getting caught and prosecuted. So while uncommon, it couldn't be ruled out.

"If this second fire is any indication, we're going to be real busy until this person is caught." Tyler made a face. "You know as well as I do, arsonists become braver with each fire. It's like they get a high and can't stop."

"Tell me about it," Mason said.

The owners of the restaurant that had been burned down earlier that week claimed that they had gotten threatening letters before the fire. Three letters over a span of the four weeks since they had opened that had warned them to close down and leave. The owners hadn't heeded the warnings, not after having invested their life's savings into the business. Then the restaurant had been burned to the ground, leaving the owners devastated.

Police were following up on leads. The suspicion being that another business owner in the area was possibly behind the arson. The letters were being analyzed for any

DNA evidence, and time would tell if they held any further clues.

With another restaurant burned to the ground and all signs pointing to arson from what Mason could tell, the idea that the culprit was another business owner—likely a restaurateur—seemed even more likely. But one could be sure.

Though early, a call to the owners of this establishment would soon take place to inform them that their restaurant had been destroyed. He wondered if the owners of this place had also gotten threatening letters.

"The scene is secure," Tyler began, "and the Fire Marshall will be here come morning. Time to head back to the station."

Mason nodded absently. Although there was a part of him that wanted to stay and examine the building, even be there when the owners arrived, he had to get his team back to the fire hall. Besides, the Fire Marshall's office would do the official investigation as to the cause of the fire. It was just that Mason was determined to find answers, which would lead to justice for the victims.

"Nothing else you can do here, man," Tyler said to him. "And once our shift is over, I don't want to hear that you came back to the scene, searching for clues."

Mason faced Tyler, who was more like a brother to him. Someone he knew would always have his back. Even if that meant intervening when he believed that Mason would spread himself too thin for the sake of a fire investigation.

"The Fire Marshall's office is perfectly capable, and you don't want to step on toes like you did last year."

Last year, Mason had inserted himself into the investigation of a warehouse fire, and had been able to find a clue in the debris that was missed. His goal had been to solve the arson, but the Fire Marshall had seen Mason as trying to one-up him, and it caused tension.

"Roberts got over it," Mason said.

"Still. Leave it to the right department. We've done our job. You might even want to spend some of your free time going on a date."

Mason scoffed. "Just because you're happily involved doesn't mean we all have to be."

"I'm just saying. Get a hobby. Find a girlfriend who lives in town. Because Kenya—she's always off jet-setting, so she can't be here to distract you."

"And she's not really my girlfriend."

"That's my point. You need to find someone. I know you, man. You have a tendency to work way too hard. The fire's out."

Mason nodded. "All right. Job well done. Let's get the guys back."

As he started back to the street with Tyler, Mason's mind was still on the situation at hand. He planned to be involved in as much of the investigation as possible on his end, no matter what Tyler said. He would do whatever it took to see the culprit caught.

As a firefighter, arson was truly the worst part of the job. Because it was a crime that destroyed people's lives. Sure, some arson cases were instances of insurance fraud, and typically in those cases no one got hurt. But Mason had seen fire used as a weapon. A weapon of hatred, a weapon of revenge, or as possibly in this case, a weapon of intimidation.

Nearly twenty years ago, fire had killed Mason's mother and his five-year-old brother. Even two decades after their deaths, Mason wondered if the fire had been arson, though it had been ruled an accident. But what had troubled Mason at the time and still haunted him today was the fact that there had been no official cause. Not a stove left on, not a cigarette burning on the sofa, not a curling iron plugged in and forgotten in the bathroom. There had been no real answers.

For Mason, who had been away at summer camp at the time, learning that his mother and brother had been killed had not only crushed him, but it had become a driving force in his life. That tragedy led him to a career in the field of fire and rescue.

He hadn't been able to save his mother and brother, and though he knew it wasn't his fault, he hadn't been able to forgive himself. Maybe he couldn't—not without real answers as to what caused the fire. What if the cause had been something that he, a fifteen-year-old boy at the time, would have been alerted to? His mother had often taken sleeping pills to calm her anxious mind, and once the fire had started she hadn't had a chance. But had he been there, Mason believed wholeheartedly that he would have smelled the smoke, heard the alarm and gotten his family to safety.

His father should have been home at the time of the fire, but instead had been out drinking with friends.

Mason flinched when he felt a hand clamp down on his shoulder. "Hey, you all right?"

Mason faced Tyler. "Yeah," he said. But he felt the tightness in his chest, one that had nothing to do with the toxic fumes the fire had produced.

Some people wondered why he had become a firefighter, given that he had been a prodigy of sorts at a young age. At the age of nineteen, Mason had been an NBA top draft pick, with a hefty contract. The eight-figure deal was the kind people could only dream of. However, five years into his career, he had walked away from it all. A controversial decision that die-hard basketball fans still talked about.

For Mason, it had been easy. Basketball had been something he was good at, but it hadn't been the burning passion in his heart.

Ever since losing his mother and brother, his heart told him that he should do something to help people. In a way, by battling every fire, he tried to atone for the fact that he wished so desperately he could turn back the clock and save his mother and brother on that terrible summer day.

Gritting his teeth, he tried to force the painful memory away. But it wasn't going anywhere. It was always there, like a physical wound that would never heal. He had learned to live with it, but the guilt prevailed.

His best friends and everyone else he knew had told him that it wasn't his fault, and rationally he knew that. He'd been a kid, needing to get away from a turbulent home by going to summer camp, the one highlight of the summer. But in retrospect, he hated that he had left his mother and little brother alone with his father, whom he'd known had always drank too much. If he hadn't gone to summer camp, wouldn't he have been able to save them that night?

It was the "what if" that continued to haunt him.

"The hoses are back on the truck," Tyler said. "The guys are ready."

Mason nodded. Then he called out to his team, "Stephenson, Eisler, Duncan. We're ready to roll out of here."

Chapter 2

Sabrina Crawford stared at the photo of Mason Foley on the screen of her Mac computer. It was a candid shot of him, taken while he was standing over a stove in the firehouse. He had been caught midlaugh, and the photo seemed to capture a confident and playful nature about him.

He was the next firefighter scheduled to come in for a photo shoot for the calendar she was working on with the Ocean City Fire Department. As she had done before each firefighter came into her studio, Sabrina checked out a candid shot of the man in order to get ideas on how best to utilize him in the shoot. Usually something about the man's eyes, smile or expression would lead to inspiration in terms of what kind of pictures she would take of him.

But right now, her mind wasn't coming up with any ideas. How could it, when all she could think about was the letter she'd received?

Glancing at the letter, which she had discarded on her desk, Sabrina swallowed. A painful lump lodged in her throat as she picked the letter up and decided to read it a second time.

Sabrina,

I am taking the time to write this letter because you are clueless. Why on earth would you think that I would ever want to hear from you? You have done enough to destroy my family. The fact that you can't even figure that out shows the kind of person you are. Selfish and horrible.

For once in your life, think about someone other than yourself! You need to stay away from me and my family. Forever. Never try to contact me again, you pitiful excuse for a human being. If you don't heed this warning, I will have to involve the authorities.

I am being as nice as I possibly can given your harassment, but none of us is interested in having anything to do with you.

You should never have been born!

Sabrina felt the same way she had when she'd read the letter half an hour earlier—as though someone had ripped her heart out of her chest. Because although the letter was unsigned, she knew who had sent it. And after simply trying to reach out to her, this awful letter was the last thing Sabrina had expected. The words made her out to be some sort of evil person. And even though she knew she wasn't the words still stung.

Especially the part about how she never should have been born. Given the circumstances under which she had come into the world that comment truly hurt.

Sabrina picked up the tension ball on her desk hoping that the stress from the back of her neck would transfer to the ball. All she had done was reach out to her sister on Facebook. She hadn't expected such a painful and rude rejection.

Though maybe she should have. Because not once in her thirty-three years had Julia and Patrick—her half siblings—ever reached out to her. Sabrina was certain that they hadn't known of her existence for several years—

as she hadn't known about them. But for the past fifteen years at least, they knew of her. Knew of her, but wanted nothing to do with her.

When Sabrina had turned eighteen, her father decided to finally introduce her to his other children. She had been nervous but hopeful. But those hopes were quickly shot down when Julia and Patrick had said less than two words upon meeting her. They'd made it clear that they wanted nothing to do with her, and that hadn't changed over the years.

It didn't take a psychologist to figure out why. Sabrina was a child of their father, conceived in an adulterous relationship. And for that reason, it seemed that they would never accept her.

It had been a huge shock to learn she had siblings, and Sabrina was sure that they were just as stunned to learn of her existence. But Sabrina acknowledged that for them, the situation had to be harder. Discovering the truth of their father's betrayal wasn't easy to accept.

Perhaps if Sabrina had never pressed the issue, she would have never known the truth about her father. But when the standard "Your father isn't in your life" answers weren't enough for her, her mother had finally told her the truth. That her father didn't live with them because he had another family. And how that family wasn't interested in getting to know her. Those had been hard words to accept at the age of thirteen, but Sabrina hadn't been concerned about people she didn't know. She'd been concerned about her father. And having another family or not, she hadn't been able to understand why he never saw her. There were other kids at her school whose parents had gone on to marry other people, but they still spent time with both parents.

Sabrina had bombarded her mother with questions about her father, and finally at the age of fifteen, her mother revealed his identity. Sabrina had been excited to find out that her father was Gerald Parker. A man her mother had been able to show her articles of in the paper, and stories about on the news. At the time she'd learned of his identity, her father had been a city councilor running for mayor. The father she had always dreamed about, had always wanted in her life, was famous. That reality had filled Sabrina with pride.

Sabrina could still remember the feeling of nervous hopefulness when her mother had arranged for her to meet him. But all the hopes and expectations she'd had of him had shattered after they'd met. Because the hope that he would become a constant figure in her life proved only to be the wishful thinking of a young girl. Even during their first meeting, Gerald Parker had seemed uncomfortable around her, and Sabrina had been smart enough to know that it wasn't simply because it was their first meeting. After that, their interactions were few and far between. He made sure to send her gifts on special occasions, but what Sabrina had wanted was his presence in her life.

As an adult, Sabrina came to understand why her mother hadn't pushed for her father to be a part of her life. Her mother knew that he would ultimately hurt her by choosing his family over her every time. For one thing, Gerald feared that the secret about his affair and illegitimate child would come out and ruin his career in politics. But Sabrina's mother, Evelyn, had never tried to do anything to hurt the man she had clearly loved. She hadn't even given Sabrina his last name, to keep anyone from learning the truth. Gerald's wife, Marilyn, who had stayed by his side despite his infidelity, wasn't able to accept the very real proof of her husband's bad behavior. At least that was what Sabrina's mother had always told her. The very few times she had seen her father proved to her the theory was true.

Sabrina hoped that her siblings—her sister in particular—might be open to a relationship with her. But clearly, that was wishful thinking.

Sabrina folded the letter, put it back in its envelope and tossed it in the top drawer of her desk. She *should* throw it out...but she would keep it as a reminder of how pointless it was to reach out to the family that wanted nothing to do with her.

Sighing, Sabrina rubbed both of her temples. As she and her mother got older, she was able to picture a future without any real family to call her own. There were cousins in upstate New York, a far cry from Ocean City where she lived. They may as well have been strangers to her. Her father and her half siblings were in the Ocean City area and Sabrina saw it as a real tragedy that she was basically banned from getting to know them.

Hadn't enough time passed to prove to Marilyn that Sabrina's mother was no longer a threat? Her mother and father had been involved thirty-four years ago. More than enough time for Marilyn Parker to put aside her gripes on getting to know Sabrina.

Through social media, Sabrina had hoped that reaching out to her sister would be the way to connect to the family that she always wanted to get to know. Neither she nor her siblings were accountable for her father's actions. They were innocent, not responsible for the way they had come into the world. Sabrina had hoped that after so many years, her siblings would be curious to get to know her and forge a relationship.

"Hey," Nya said softly, peaking her head into the office. "Can I come in?"

Sabrina looked up at her office assistant and best friend, whom she had known since high school.

"Sure," Sabrina told Nya.

"Well?" Nya asked cautiously as she walked into the

office. "I figure if it was good news, you would have told me. I've been patiently waiting, giving you time. But now I'm figuring you might need a hug."

"She wants nothing to do with," Sabrina said simply.

Nya sat in the chair opposite Sabrina's desk. "That's all she said?"

"Her language was a bit more colorful."

Nya searched Sabrina's desk. "Where's the letter? Did you throw it out?"

"I should have. But I put it in my desk."

"Can I read it?"

Sabrina opened the desk and retrieved the letter, and then passed it to Nya. Her best friend for fifteen years, Sabrina shared everything with Nya. She couldn't really talk to her mother about this, because her mother would surely say I told you so. Especially since her mother had told her for years that her father's family would never come around.

Nya withdrew the letter from the envelope. Sabrina could tell when she got to the more vile parts because her eyes began to bulge.

"Oh, my God. This is her reply?"

"Like I said, it's obvious that she wants nothing to do with me."

"Still, this isn't the way to respond to people. I saw the message you sent her on Facebook. You were very polite. Overly polite. It did not call for this kind of a response."

Sabrina nodded. She realized she was gritting her teeth, and made a deliberate attempt to relax her jaw, shoulders, and the rest of her body. "Obviously, there's nothing I can do about this. I held this dream for too long."

"Well, I say forget them." Nya shoved the letter back into the envelope. "You don't get to choose your family, but thankfully, you do get to choose your friends." She beamed, and gestured to herself. "And this friend would love to take you out for dinner and drinks tonight so we can forget this letter ever arrived. What do you say?"

"I don't know, Nya. I was kind of thinking I would just chill out tonight. Probably watch one of those Chevy Chase movies to remind me that families are overrated." She smiled, but knew it had come off as forced.

"No. You are not going to stay home and wallow. Who needs Julia Parker when you have Nya Hayes? Better than any blood sister could ever be."

Sabrina cracked a real smile this time. Nya was right about one thing, you didn't get to choose your family. At least Sabrina had chosen wisely when she had befriended the scrawny girl with braces her senior year of high school. At the time, Nya had been new to the school, and it was hard to make friends when you were the new kid. Sabrina knew something about feeling as though you didn't fit in, and she and Nya had become fast friends. Nya had since blossomed into a beautiful woman—with perfect teeth.

Nya was still looking for love, like Sabrina. So Sabrina knew that as much as Nya enjoyed going out for dinner or a drink with a friend, she also hoped that she would spot her Mr. Right. And it was that part of a night out that Sabrina wasn't looking forward to.

Sabrina loved Nya dearly, but wasn't in the mood to hear her rate various men, nor watch her flirt. Nya was like a sister to her, but in that way, they were as different as night and day. Nya was prone to looking for love around every corner and as Sabrina sometimes joked, under every rock. But after Sabrina's failed marriage, she wasn't looking for any man at all.

Though, if God were to appear before her and tell her that a certain man was the right one, she wouldn't ignore that type of divine intervention. But for now, she was happy concentrating on her work as a photographer, which kept her very busy. And in this competitive field, she didn't have much time to think about marriage or family. She was happy to focus solely on her career and expanding her clientele.

Over the past seven years, Sabrina had created a name for herself as a skilled wedding and special events photographer. It was her reputation that had led her to get what she considered a dream assignment. She was contracted to take photos of the local firemen at Station Two in downtown Ocean City for their annual firefighter calendar fund-raiser.

"And we can make it a business meeting, if you want," Nya said. "I would love to see the shots you've taken of the first five firemen."

Sabrina looked at her friend and grinned. "I'm sure you would." But Sabrina was funny that way. She didn't want anyone seeing her work until she was satisfied with it. From taking the shots to determining which ones were best, she was a consummate professional who trusted her eye and her eye alone. "You know I will let you see every single shot—once I have determined which ones are the best."

Nya frowned. "Come on. I'm a hot-blooded, single female. I think I can help you determine which shots are the best."

"You know how I work," Sabrina said. "Besides, if I leave it to you, you'll have all the raciest photos in the calendar—which is not necessarily what the fire station wants."

"Racy sells!" Nya objected. "I saw the calendar they put out last year." She frowned. "It was okay, but it could've been a lot better."

"Which is why they hired me for the job." Sabrina had taken the initiative to go to the fire station and offer her services as photographer for the next calendar. She'd brought a portfolio of her work, had talked to them about her creative ideas to make the calendar better and assured them she could produce a stunning calendar that would sell. She had obviously impressed the powers that be at the station, because they had given her the job. And along with it, a very attractive fee.

"It's going to be a great calendar," Sabrina said. Over the past week and a half a handful of the firefighters had come in as their schedules allowed. Firefighter Mason Foley was scheduled to come in the next afternoon, and she was looking forward to the shoot.

She had taken photos at the fire station already, and other places. But she had something else in mind for Mason. Perhaps along a stretch of beach or someplace with a scenic background. She was glad that he had hours to spend with her because she had a few locations in mind that would highlight the beauty of Ocean City. And most importantly, the brave men who worked to keep not only fire under control, but who also rescued people in car accidents and a number of other situations. The Ocean City Fire Department was all encompassing, and fires were really only a small percentage of the job they did.

"You know you don't want to wallow in misery on your sofa this evening, especially not before your shoot tomorrow. And what better way to keep me distracted from the eye candy in the restaurant than to show me the pictures you've taken so far?"

Sabrina narrowed her eyes. "Oh, you're good."

Nya tapped a finger against her cheek. "What better way to kill two birds with one stone? Lighten your mood, and keep me from flirting with the available men?"

That remained to be seen, but Sabrina was already sold. Why not? She made the rules, so she could certainly break a few now and then.

"All right," Sabrina began, "I'll bring the laptop and

let you see some of the shots I took of the first firefighter, Alex. I want to go over those with a fresh eye, anyway."

Nya squealed. "Oh, I can't wait!"

Chapter 3

Sabrina held the receiver to her ear and listened to the phone as it rang. On the third ring, she was pretty certain that Mason Foley wasn't going to pick up.

Again.

She had already left him two messages to confirm their appointment, but he hadn't gotten back to her. Now, she had no clue if he was going to show that afternoon.

"How unprofessional can a person be?" she muttered, and pulled the phone away from her ear to hang up. She halted. Had she just heard someone say something on the other end of the line?

Quickly, she brought the phone back to her ear, still uncertain if she had heard anything other than the beginning of Mason's voicemail greeting.

"Hello?" said the groggy voice.

"Oh, hi," Sabrina said lamely. She had expected no response and wasn't actually prepared to speak to the man.

"Yes?" Mason said.

"Oh, I'm sorry. Did I wake you?"

She heard him yawn before saying, "It's okay. Who's calling?"

Sabrina glanced at the clock on her computer screen. It was minutes after ten in the morning—a time when most people were up. But Mason was a firefighter, and she knew that they worked twenty-four hour shifts. It was likely that he had worked the night before and barely had a full night of rest.

Either that or he had spent the night pleasuring a woman. She'd seen his picture, and just looking at his gorgeous face and immaculately toned body, she knew he was the type who had to fight them off.

"Hello?"

"Um, this is Sabrina Crawford," Sabrina quickly said, wondering why her thoughts had ventured to Mason's likely night of making love. "I'm the photographer working on the Firefighter's Calendar. I'm sorry to call so early. But you're supposed to come in today for your shoot."

"Yeah, that's right."

What did that mean? "So you're going to make it?" Sabrina asked.

"Yeah, I'll be there."

"Oh. Oh, good."

"Why do you sound surprised?"

"Well, I wasn't sure. I left you a couple of messages to confirm, and I didn't hear back from you."

"Sorry about that. I've been busy with work. I meant to call you back, but didn't get around to it."

"It's fine," she told him. At least she'd gotten through, because she had started to worry that he would be a no-show. "So today at three o'clock?"

"Actually, is there a chance we can do it a bit later?"

"How much later?"

"Like four p.m. I had a late night due to a fire. You may have heard about it. The restaurant on Maple Avenue. And I'd like to head into the firehouse before seeing you. I need to follow up on something."

"Four o'clock will be fine. Again, I'm sorry I woke you up."

"No problem."

"Just to confirm, you're bringing your fire gear including helmet, as well as your dress uniform."

"Yep. I'll bring some tools, as well. Accessories for the shoot."

"Sounds great," Sabrina said. "I'll see you at four."

Sabrina hung up. She then loaded up a picture of Mason on her screen. It became all too clear why she had thought about him in bed. He was gorgeous, and everything about him oozed sex appeal, which would work out well for her shoot. She was certain that he would be an easy model to work with.

With each of the firefighters, she had taken shots of them in her studio. She also taken some photos at the firehouse with the engine and ladder trucks as backdrops but she had also utilized local parks, the waterfront, and the forest the bordered the eastern side of town. With Mason, she wanted to travel a little bit north along a stretch of the Pacific Ocean that had a beautiful rocky backdrop. She was certain to capture what would be stunning photographs there. She wanted the calendar to be pleasing not only because of the male models, but because of the lush scenery in Ocean City. It was what would make this particular calendar unique.

And he had a feeling that Mason was going to be an ideal model.

It was just minutes before four o'clock when Nya entered Sabrina's studio to announce that Mason Foley had arrived.

"Oh, good." Sabrina climbed down from the stepladder. She had just finished putting up the background she wanted to start with for the shoot. It was a cityscape of Ocean City at night. Turning to face Nya, she saw a huge grin on her friend's face.

"Nya, what is it?"

"Giiirl." Nya all but pranced toward her, the grin on her face growing even bigger. "I have seen some fine men in my day, but Mason— Oh, my Lord. He has got to be *the* finest man to step foot in this studio!"

Sabrina looked beyond Nya's shoulder toward the door that led out of the studio, in case Mason had followed her in. Not seeing him, she said in a lowered voice, "So the man is fine. Get a hold of yourself."

"That's easy for you to say. You haven't seen him yet! I'm just trying to prepare you!"

"Okay, I get it." Sabrina sounded nonchalant. She had photographed all sorts of people in her life. She wasn't the type to lose her head over an attractive man. "Go ahead and tell him to come on back. I'm ready for him."

"Oh, you think you're ready."

What the heck had gotten into Nya? "You know what you need?" Sabrina said, smiling sweetly. "You need a man." It was obvious that her friend had gone too long since her last relationship, because her extreme reaction to this Mason guy was over the top. Sabrina only hoped that Nya had been professional with Mason in the reception area.

"Maybe I can help you here while you do the shoot?" Nya offered.

"Nya!" Sabrina made a face. "What's gotten into you?"

Sabrina shooed her silently, hoping that Mason had not overheard any of their conversation. She had to admit that this behavior was a little out of character, even for man-crazed Nya.

And it wasn't that Sabrina didn't enjoy a good-looking man as much as the next woman, but she certainly knew how to be professional.

"Go get him, please," Sabrina reiterated. "And please be professional," she added in a hushed voice.

Once Nya left the room, Sabrina went over to the octagonal softbox light that she had set up, and fussed with it. She heard his footsteps, but still didn't look behind her, preferring to appear busy.

"Ms. Crawford?"

Sabrina turned. And just like that, the air left her lungs in a rush. Instantly, she understood why Nya had been out of sorts. Mason Foley was indeed a stunningly gorgeous man.

When Sabrina had seen his picture on her computer, she had deemed him to be a fine specimen of a man. One who would surely be a hit with the ladies when the calendar was produced. In fact, she had already figured that a picture with him would be great on the cover.

But her reaction to him now was visceral. And for a moment, she was bereft of words.

Totally unlike her.

He took a step into her studio, seeming to fill the space with his tall muscular frame. "You're Ms. Crawford, right?"

It was then that Sabrina realized that she had not moved since seeing him, and she forced one foot in front of the other until she reached him. She outstretched her hand and offered him a smile. "Sorry. I just…" She just what? Was taken aback by his good looks? Surely she couldn't tell him that. "I didn't expect that you would be so tall," she finally said. "How tall *are* you?"

"Six foot six," he told her.

"Oh, wow." Realizing that her tone had been filled with awe, Sabrina frowned slightly. What was wrong with her? She felt flushed, and her heart was beating faster than normal. It had been a long time since just looking at a man had set her heart aflutter like this.

The pictures she had seen of him did him no justice. In person, there was a quality to him that radiated throughout the room. A charisma that made him instantly likable.

Glancing beyond Mason, she saw that Nya was standing in the doorway, a dreamy look on her face. Sabrina cleared her throat before speaking. "Nya, would you put the kettle on?" She faced Mason. "Would you like some tea, coffee, water? We also have a variety of juice."

"Just a bottle of water, that'd be great."

"Is there anything else I can get for you?" Nya asked. "I can run out and get some sweets from the bakery across the street, if you like…"

Sabrina widened her eyes as Mason turned to look at Nya, silently trying to tell her friend to take it easy.

"Just the water," Mason told her.

And when he turned back to look at Sabrina, she felt a definite charge. Goodness, it wasn't simply that he was good-looking. What Sabrina felt was undeniable attraction for this man.

She turned, walking toward the backdrop, determined to rid herself of whatever had taken over her being. "You brought your gear?" she asked.

"Yes. It's in the reception area. I figured I would ask you how you want to do this first. You might want to take a couple of shots of me wearing this before I change."

Mason was wearing jeans and a white cotton shirt that was unbuttoned down to his mid chest with the sleeves rolled up. There was an easy confidence to the way he walked, and Sabrina got the sense that he knew exactly how he affected women.

Sabrina could easily take photos of him in what he was wearing, and probably make a fortune selling them to *GQ* magazine. But this shoot was for the firefighter's calendar, and that meant taking photos of him in his uniform. In full gear, partial gear and in his dress uniform. She would take a variety of pictures and decide which ones were best. But if he looked as good without his shirt on as she expected, she had a feeling that the best photos of

Mason would be ones with him wearing only his fire re-
tardant pants and suspenders. She was certain those would
be a hit with the women.

"Actually, if you could show me what you brought, that
would be great." She spoke the words and knew that her
voice sounded a little wispy. "We can decide from there
what's best for you to wear, but I definitely want you in
your uniform." She paused. "How do you feel about going
shirtless?"

"I have no problem with it. I'm yours to do with as you
please."

Sabrina had to do everything in her power not to react
with a sound of carnal lust. The suggestive nature of what
he'd said had her coming undone.

Which was ridiculous. Obviously, his words hadn't had
any secret meaning. She had seen many attractive men before, photographed plenty of them. Why was she so flustered around this one?

"It'll all be tasteful, of course. And as long as you look
good with your shirt off, I'm sure the shots will come out
great." She smiled. "Oh, there's Nya with your water. I'm
not sure if I actually introduced you, but Nya is my personal assistant and also one of my best friends. So anything you need, feel free to ask her."

Nya approached him with the bottle of water, her eyes
wide, as though she were a deer caught in headlights.

"Thank you," Mason said as he accepted the bottle of
water.

As he took it in his left hand, Sabrina surreptitiously
checked out his ring finger. It was bare.

Nya continued to stare, and Mason gave her an odd
look. "I—I'm sorry that I'm staring. It's just that I don't
see men like you coming into the studio."

Sabrina narrowed her eyes. "Forgive my assistant—"

"It's just that you're so tall."

"Six foot six."

"And you went into firefighting instead of basketball?" Nya shook her head, as though she couldn't understand what he had been thinking.

"Nya," Sabrina said. "Can you please call back the Johnsons to make sure they got my message about changing their appointment time?"

"Of course," she said. Then, to Mason, "You're sure I can't get you anything else?"

"We're fine," Sabrina said, her tone firm.

"Okay. Well, you know where I am if you need me." Nya's smile was syrupy as she stepped backward out of the studio, before finally turning and heading toward the front office.

"All right." She faced Mason again. "If you'd put on your entire outfit, helmet and all, that would be good." She figured it would be best to start with him in his full uniform, and then he could take off the layers, as she deemed necessary.

"Sounds good. Where should I get changed?"

"When you go back out to the front, you're going to see a door on your left. That's the washroom. Feel free to get changed in there. Or, if you need more space, I can let you get changed in here and I can wait out front until you're ready. Whichever works best for you."

"I'll figure it out."

As Mason headed out of the studio, Sabrina couldn't help eyeing his long, muscular frame.

She then mentally reprimanded herself for being so distracted by the man's good looks and made her way over to her Canon 5D. She checked to make sure that the battery was full, which she knew it was. However, she had others in the room charged and ready to go if that one lost power. Then she went to her camera bag and verified that all of the accessories she would need for their trip to the beach were indeed there.

When Mason came back into the studio dressed in his fireman's uniform, Sabrina felt the same bodily reaction toward him as she had earlier. Obviously, it had been way too long since she had been involved with anyone. But he was definitely not her type, so her pull of attraction toward him made no sense.

He took a step toward her, and her pulse sped up. Okay, so she was lying to herself. The man was definitely her type. In terms of the kind of man that turned her on, Mason may as well be pictured in the dictionary. But he was also the kind of man who turned on lots of women, and Sabrina was wise enough to know that that kind of guy was dangerous to a girl's heart.

Her heart in particular.

She'd dated the kind of man that everyone liked back in college, and had ended up heartbroken because of it. She had long since vowed never to date someone that every woman had to stop and gawk at ever again.

"What do you think?" he asked.

That was a loaded question. She thought he was smoking hot. He would look—at least for the calendar—like the hero he was. A man in uniform here to rescue the damsel in distress.

"Looks great." She averted her eyes. "Why don't you come up in front of the canvas? I like this one, and I've got plenty more that we can try, as well. Let's start with some shots of you in your full uniform like this, and then we can go to shots where you take off the upper portion. You know, give the ladies what they want."

Mason's smile was enigmatic. And, if she wasn't mistaken, it was a smile just for her.

Again looking away from him, she first closed the door to the studio for privacy, and then headed toward her camera. He walked past her and stood in front of the wall where the canvas was set up. Sabrina looked through the lens of her Canon, getting a sense of how she wanted the photo to be framed. She manually zoomed the lens out to see his entire body, and then half pressed the shutter release button to focus the shot. Easing her head back, she eyed the lights that she had set up on either side of the room, satisfied that they needed no adjustments. She snapped off a test shot, and looked at the viewfinder to see how she liked it.

"I wasn't ready," Mason said playfully.

"That was just a test shot, but you look great. You're a natural."

Mason was definitely one of the most photogenic men she had ever come across.

"Okay, keep standing the way you are. But look at the camera. And don't smile. Give me a serious face." Mason did as she asked, and she snapped shot after shot. "Good, let's do a couple more just like that. Turn your head slightly to the left. No, my left." She grinned. Then she took a couple more pictures. From her viewfinder, she was very impressed with the results. "Excellent. Now, how about you give me a smile?"

Mason's smile was instant, and it lit up the room. He looked good in his more serious shots, as well, but his smile was like a giant gold foil bow on a Christmas present—the perfect final touch on an extravagant package.

Sabrina took photo after photo of Mason in his full uniform. Then she had him hold his helmet against his chest for some of the pictures, and under his arm, as well. Almost all of the shots looked great. It was going to be hard to choose the right one, but that was a good dilemma.

Now it was time to get a little sexier.

"As we discussed, you can take off the upper portion of your uniform. I'm going to change the backdrop." She had ordered a backdrop from a photo she had taken of flames, and she loved how it turned out. She went across the room to the far wall to get the stool so that she could use it to unhook the current backdrop. She looked in Mason's direction, surprised that he had begun to disrobe right there, instead of heading to the bathroom. She caught a glimpse of his smooth dark skin, and quickly averted her gaze. Mostly. But she couldn't quite help glancing in his direction.

"Do you want some help?" he asked.

"No," Sabrina responded. She had pulled the lever to wind up the canvas, and it was ready to come down. "I generally don't put the talent to work."

"That's not what I call work. I've got no problem helping you do this. What do you need to do? Unhook it?"

"It's okay." Sabrina stretched to reach the top portion of the heavy canvas, and when she looked down, Mason was at her side. "Certainly you're not opposed to someone helping you? And for what it's worth, I don't consider myself the talent. We're in this together, aren't we? You're helping the fire station create a great calendar that's going to bring us lots of money, which, of course, is going to help out local charities. Let me help you do this, even if you are completely capable of doing it yourself."

Sabrina looked down at him. The glimpse of his hard muscles and strong arms made her suck in a breath. He extended his hand to her, and she took it, feeling a zap of heat as he helped her down from the stool.

"Thank you," she said. "And once that's down, I'm going to put up the canvas that's resting in the corner." She pointed to it.

"No problem."

Sabrina watched as he easily put up the next backdrop for her.

Finished, he said, "There you go."

"Thank you," she told him.

Mason gestured to his upper body with a hand as he walked toward her. "So, does my chest meet with your approval?"

Sabrina's eyes bulged. She wasn't even sure how to answer.

"Do I look good with my shirt off?" he added.

And then she remembered the comment she had made earlier, and understood. "Oh, of course. Yes—"

"You seemed to be concerned that I might not be up to snuff," he said, his lips curling in a grin. "So that's why I was wondering. I want to make sure that you think I'm up to standard for the calendar."

Sabrina swallowed. Surely he was joking or perhaps searching for a compliment. But his body—with an eight-pack and hard planes and muscles in all the right places—was more than satisfactory for the calendar.

It was phenomenal.

In fact, she was almost certain now that he would be the model she used for the front cover.

"I'm not sure why I said what I did," Sabrina explained. "It was an off-the-cuff remark. Certainly unfounded. Your chest is flawless."

"Thanks," he said, his eyes twinkling as he smiled down at her.

Was he flirting with her, or was she out of her mind? Maybe her libido was simply clouding the sense God had given her.

There was a knock at the door, and Sabrina turned. "Come in," she called.

Nya opened the door, and her eyes instantly went to Mason, sweeping over his naked upper body. Her expression said that she liked very much what she saw.

"Oh, wow." She couldn't hide her wanton appreciation of Mason's body. Her eyes steadfast on him, she said, "Sorry to disturb you, but it's after five, so I was going to head out. I've got that date to get ready for. But I wanted to see if you need anything else from me first."

"I'm fine." Sabrina turned to Mason. "You need anything?"

Mason shook his head. "Nope."

When Sabrina looked at Nya again, she saw that her friend was still gawking at Mason, as though he was a public display of priceless art. Sabrina began to walk toward her. "We were going to head out soon, anyway, so feel free to head on home," she said when she reached her friend. She then took Nya by the arm and physically led her out of the studio. Nya craned her head over her shoulder to say, "Bye, Mason. It was nice to meet you."

"Nya, what's gotten into you?" Sabrina asked once they reached the front office.

"Are you kidding me? That is one of the finest men I have ever seen."

"Yes, he is. But remember, I run a professional studio here. I don't want him thinking that he can't be comfortable taking off his shirt."

"I know, I know. But damn, he is *fine*. I can't wait to see those photos." Nya paused. "Did you find out if he's single?"

"Nya! Aren't you going on a date this evening?"

"Hmm, are you getting a little territorial?" Nya's eyes narrowed as a look of playful curiosity crossed her face. "You like him, don't you?" It was more of a statement, than a question. "Yes, you do!"

"He's an attractive guy, sure, but am I supposed to be losing my mind over him?"

"I know you," Nya began. "Look at you, there's actually a bit of a spark in your eyes! Thank God, because I was beginning to wonder if you were dead from the waist down."

Sabrina placed her hands on her hips and frowned. "Nya, this is completely inappropriate."

"Look, I just wanted to know. Because if you're not interested, and my date tonight doesn't go well, then I'd love to get to know Mr. Firefighter better. But I can tell you like him, so I'll back off."

Sabrina stared at her friend in complete shock. "I don't even want to know what you're going on about. Mason is here to take photos. This is all about business."

Nya looked at her, raising an eyebrow. "Maybe it should be about a little pleasure, as well. After all, you haven't even dated since your divorce."

"Okay, that's enough." Sabrina spoke sweetly. "Get your bag." Once Nya had her purse slung over her shoulder, Sabrina put her hand on her back and guided her toward the front door. "I'll see you tomorrow."

"Go for it," Nya told her before Sabrina closed the door and locked it.

Through the glass, Nya held her gaze, giving her a thumbs-up gesture to imply that she had meant what she'd said.

Sabrina flipped the CLOSED sign on her door and turned away from her friend who was still beckoning at her in sign language.

Nya had clearly lost her mind.

Chapter 4

With Nya gone, Sabrina headed back into her studio. There, she found Mason texting on his smartphone. When he saw her walk in, he slipped the phone into his pocket and faced her. And for some reason, Sabrina's mood went down a notch. Had he just been texting a girlfriend?

What did it matter if he had been? Maybe Nya's nonsensical talk had gotten into her psyche, because it didn't make sense that she should care about whomever he was texting. Just because he was an attractive man didn't mean she had to act on what she was feeling. Even if her heart was racing simply from being in the same room with him.

She almost laughed at the thought that had entered her head. Was she actually thinking that Mason might go for someone like her? Not that she wasn't an attractive woman. She had certainly had her fair share of attention from men. But guys like Mason—men who were in another league of hot—went for a specific type. And she wasn't it. She didn't dress to show her sexuality, she didn't wear makeup to highlight every feature. She wasn't Plain Jane, but she was fairly conservative. She pegged Mason for the kind of man who went after the hottest women. Women who loved to wear revealing clothing and parade themselves as eye candy. Sabrina was definitely not that kind of woman.

Pushing any ridiculous thought about dating out of her mind, she faced Mason and said, "You all set?"

"Ready when you are."

Sabrina instructed him to stand in front of the new backdrop, and then she went back to work, taking picture after picture. The backdrop of the flames looked amazing, and the contrast of his dark skin against the bright reds and oranges of the fire was striking.

She stepped away from the camera and walked toward a shelf where she kept supplies. She picked up a spray bottle filled with a concoction of water and baby oil and started toward him. "I'd like your chest to be glistening for these shots. As though you've just finished battling a fire, and you're sweating. Do you mind if I spray something on your chest? It's water and baby oil."

"You can do whatever you'd like with me," he said, his grin both sexy and playful.

She tried her best not to show a reaction and approached him. She sprayed his chest, and he flinched. "Too cold?"

"No, it's fine."

She continued to spray his chest. She then smoothed her hand over one of his biceps, spreading the mix. And though she was the consummate professional, she couldn't deny the rush of heat she felt just by touching his body. He felt incredible. Strong and powerful. Tipping up on her toes, she stretched to rub her hand over his shoulder.

"I usually don't let a woman grope me like this until the second date."

Sabrina's face flushed, and she halted.

Mason chortled. "I'm just messing with you."

Of course he was, so why did she feel so ruffled? It had to be the feel of his amazing body, and the undeniable sexual charge she felt.

Once she made sure his other arm was adequately glistening, she returned the bottle to the shelf, dried her hands with a towel, and took her position behind the camera. Over the next twenty minutes, she took a good hundred pictures.

"I think I've got all that I need in here. I'd love to head to the beach, as I mentioned before. The spot I've picked is about fifteen minutes away. I think it's perfect. We can go in my SUV, and then I can bring you back. I figure it's best if you just stay in your uniform. Obviously, you can put your shirt back on for now. I've got towels in the bathroom you can dry off with. When we get to the beach, I'd love to get shots of you with the T-shirt and suspenders, as well. But definitely also more shots of you without your shirt on."

"Fine with me," Mason said, "but if you don't mind, I would prefer to take my car and follow you. I'll have to get going once we finish at the beach."

"Oh." Sabrina nodded. "Sure. That's fine."

She already had her camera bag pretty much set. But she dismounted her Canon 5D from her tripod, put it in its case and added it to the bag. In the meantime, Mason put on his shirt and gathered his own belongings.

Minutes later, they were heading out the door.

"My car's in the back. I'll drive around to the front. I'll be in a red Chevy Equinox."

"And that's my car right there." Mason pointed to the sleek black Mercedes, the CLS version of the car that came with a hefty price tag. She knew that from having dated a real estate agent who had driven the exact same car, except in white.

It affirmed for her that Mason liked flashy cars—and by extension, flashy women.

Sabrina headed toward Pacific Coast Highway. She took it north until she reached the exit that would take her to the stretch of beach she wanted. It tended to be quieter than other spots along the Pacific, which was ideal.

As she searched for parking, she spied Mason's vehicle behind hers. She had offered him a ride in her vehicle, but now she was thinking that it was best that he had not come with her, after all. Something about her session with him still had her heart beating a little faster than normal, and she couldn't help thinking that Nya was right.

She had come alive in a way that was shocking. For the past two years, she had been all about her career. Her marriage had failed in large part because her husband had not been able to deal with her being a career woman.

She parked at a meter on the street where two spots were available, and Mason parked alongside her. Then she got out of her truck, opened the back and began to unload her camera bag.

"Here." Mason, who was suddenly beside her, spoke. "Let me help you with your stuff."

He had his own bag with gear, yet took hers, as well, before she could take it out of the trunk. She grabbed the portable stand and umbrella setup for her Quantum Q flash, which she would need in order to erase any shadows as she took pictures of Mason facing the water. She also grabbed her tripod.

"This is a heavy bag," Mason commented. "What do you have in it?"

"Two of everything," she said. "A couple different types of flashes, extra batteries, different lenses, a variety of filters. Pretty much everything I need in order to shoot away from my studio."

"And where are we heading?"

"Straight ahead. To those steps that lead down to the beach."

It was the first weekend in June, and the beach was sparsely populated, unlike the weekend before. For the Memorial Day weekend, Sabrina had headed to this beach with Nya, thinking it would be quiet, but it had been jam packed with people.

Thankfully, today the closest people to where she

planned to set up were a good fifty yards away, allowing for privacy.

Forty-five minutes after arriving at the beach, Sabrina
told Mason that they were done. She was beyond satisfied
with the shots. With the rocks as a backdrop, the beach,
and the stretch of Pacific, they all looked stunning. Mason
would certainly be a top contender for the front cover, but
she would finalize that once all the photos had been taken
of the remaining firefighters. There were still five more
to go. But with his status as captain at the station, it made
sense that he be featured.

She was elated that everything had gone so well, and
hated for the shoot to be done because Mason had been
incredibly easy to work with.

"All right," Sabrina announced. "I think I have everything I need. Thank you for a great shoot. I know the pictures are going to be amazing."

"I had fun," Mason said.

Sabrina disassembled her umbrella light, folded the tripod and light stand, and returned everything to her camera
bag. Mason was stripping out of his fire pants and boots
while she packed up. Once he had the pants off, Sabrina's
eyes ventured to his bare feet. Good grief, even his feet
looked sexy. From her vantage point, they looked long and
perfectly formed. Manly.

While Sabrina figured out a way to juggle all of the
items she'd brought, Mason came over to her and extended
a hand. "Let me take your bag," he offered.

"I got it," she told him, finally securing the light stand
and tripod under each arm, the camera bag already slung
over her shoulder.

"I can see that. But I'm offering to help you."

"And I appreciate it, but I've carried my camera bag and
gear around a gazillion times. I don't need—"

"Are you always this stubborn?" Mason asked.

"Stubborn? I wouldn't call it stubborn because I'm used to handling myself in all types of photo shoot situations. It comes with the territory." Besides, for some reason, she was ready for Mason to be on his way. The sooner the better.

"And I like being a gentleman. Come on, give me one of the bags."

Looking at him, Sabrina conceded. The car was parked a good ways down the street and the gear was heavy. She passed him the large bag.

"I can take the tripod, as well," Mason said.

"I—" She stopped herself midprotest, and said, "All right." She gave him a sidelong glance as she looked up at him. "I guess I am a bit stubborn. But I've always been used to taking care of myself."

"And why is that? No man to take care of you?"

Sabrina stopped and looked up at him. "I don't need a man to take care of me."

"So that's it."

"You make it sound like a curse."

"It's neither good nor bad. But perhaps you can tell me all about it over dinner."

Sabrina's eyes widened. Had she just heard Mason correctly? She decided that even if she had, it had been a slip of the tongue on his part.

She began to walk briskly, thanks to the fact that she was no longer weighed down by her heavy bag.

"That was a question. Customarily, questions are followed by an answer."

Sabrina turned around to face Mason, who was looking at her with a disarming grin. "You were serious?"

"Of course I was serious. I'd love to take you to dinner. I can't do it tonight, but perhaps we can make arrangements for tomorrow. I'm back to work on Friday."

"No, thank you," Sabrina said without preamble.

"Just like that? You're not even going to consider it?"

Sabrina hesitated before speaking. She was trying to digest the fact that Mason had even asked her out when she was certain she wasn't his type. "This isn't uncommon," she said after a moment. "Feeling close to someone after spending some time in a photo shoot."

Mason's laughter was instant. "Are you saying that in the last two hours, you think I've developed some sort of savior complex where you're concerned? Or do you call it a photographer's complex? I'm not familiar with the term."

Sabrina inhaled a breath and continued. After hearing Mason's response, she conceded that the idea sounded a little silly. But she persisted, nonetheless. "To a degree, yes. We connected well. We enjoyed some flirtatious banter. I've seen you with your shirt off. I even rubbed your body down with that solution. And now you think it would be a nice idea to take me on a date."

Mason looked amused. "So you're telling me that hitting on the photographer who just took photos of me is typical?"

Sabrina was flustered once again. She hadn't exactly come off as eloquently as she'd hoped to. But he had to understand the idea that she was getting at. That simply because they had spent time together, he was feeling that they'd connected. That was what was making him think that going on a date would be a good idea. But whatever attraction he was feeling wasn't really founded in reality.

"It's not an official complex or anything," Sabrina said, not quite meeting his eyes. "Just…you know how people who work together often end up dating? Simply because they spend so much time together during the work week. That's sort of what I'm getting at."

"Ahhh."

"And typically, they end up regretting it."

"Right."

Thank God, he understood.

"Thanks for the warning," Mason went on. "I appreciate your consideration for not wanting to blur the lines between business and pleasure, if that's what this is. But all the same, my reason for asking you out has nothing to do with the fact that you've seen me with my shirt off. Plenty of people have seen me with my shirt off, and I didn't ask them out on a date."

Sabrina's face flamed. "Like I said, that came out the wrong way."

Then she started walking again, grateful that Mason did the same, in silence. At her SUV, Mason helped her get the bags into her trunk. Sabrina was ready to be on her way and forget about this strange interaction with Mason.

Until he said, "Despite what you said, I actually would like to take you out to dinner. Would tomorrow work for you?"

Sabrina looked up at him, shocked. So he was serious. This wasn't going according to plan, not at all. She was truly hoping that they could simply part ways, so she could put the unprofessional parts of the day out of her mind.

"Why?" she found herself asking.

"Call me old school, but I'd like to take you to dinner because I find you incredibly attractive and I'd like to get to know you better."

His words stumped her. She hadn't expected him to say that. He was way too gorgeous to be single, let alone interested in her.

"Mason, I'm flattered, but—"

"Don't say no. I'll take you somewhere nice, we'll enjoy a delicious dinner and we'll talk."

"I'm flattered, I really am. But I'm sorry. I—I'm just not interested."

Mason looked at her, his eyes narrowing with suspicion. "Oh. You're involved with someone?"

"Do I have to be involved with someone to say no to

you?" Sabrina asked. She crossed her arms over her chest, unaware of the defensive gesture.

"That would be one explanation."

She laughed without mirth. "Quite the ego you have, don't you?"

"Maybe I'm completely off base, but I thought I felt something between us. Some sparks. Especially…"

"Especially what?"

"Especially when you had your hands on my body."

Sabrina felt a rush of heat, which she attributed to embarrassment. "Really? Well, you couldn't be more wrong."

"Oh. *Ohhh.*" Mason's eyes widened, as if he finally understood something. "Are you telling me that you're not into men?"

For a moment, Sabrina was too speechless to react. Then her lips parted, and she gaped at him. "Because I'm not interested in going out with you, that means I'm *gay?*"

"It's a possibility."

Sabrina was suddenly enraged. There was a part of her that wanted to throttle him. He was smiling good-naturedly, as if this was all just fun and games for him.

"No, I'm not gay. I don't appreciate your caveman tactics. If no one has ever had the guts to tell you no before, let me be the first one."

Instead of being frazzled by her comment, Mason's eyes lit up with humor. "Caveman?"

"Well, you certainly seem to have Neanderthal attitudes about dating."

"Caveman, Neanderthal. Go ahead, don't hold back. Tell me what you really feel."

Sabrina gritted her teeth, and then closed the door to the back of her vehicle. She was beyond ready to get out of there.

She went to the driver's-side door, but Mason followed

her. "Are you planning to take off? Without even a good-bye?"

"You are getting on my last nerve," she muttered.

"What was that?" he asked.

Sabrina spun around to face him. "You want to know what I think about you? I think you're attractive man. One who has an honorable job. But a guy like you has a hard time hearing *no*. And because no one tells you no, you expect everyone you ask out to say yes. Right now, you're completely baffled as to how I could possibly reject you. So you assume I must be gay. That's why I said you have a caveman attitude. It is offensive for you to assume that I'm not interested men, simply because I'm not interested in you."

"I don't think anyone has ever called me a caveman before."

"I call it as I see it. And with your archaic—"

Before Sabrina even knew what was happening, Mason suddenly bent down, slipped his arms around the back of her knees and hoisted her over his shoulder.

Sabrina screamed. "What are you doing?" she demanded.

"I'm going to take you somewhere so I can have my wicked way with you."

"Let me down!"

"Why? According to you, this is how I operate, right?"

Sabrina could see people's heads whipping in her direction, smirks across their faces. Two people who had just exited a car nearby raised their cell phones and began snapping pictures.

"This is humiliating!" Sabrina went on.

"But I'm only doing what you expect of me. You said I'm a Neanderthal. In fact, you said that about three times."

"Let me down!"

"Not until you take back what you said."

"Mason! I swear—"

He then slowly slipped her down his body. Her breasts pressed against his rock-hard chest as he lowered her. Her heart was racing, her pulse pounding in her ears. She gripped his shoulders instinctively, for balance, but the moment her feet hit the ground, she pounded on his chest.

She should have slapped him, but he had already made a spectacle of her and she didn't want to draw more attention to them.

"How could you?" she asked, her chest heaving up and down. "People are staring! Taking pictures! I'm probably going to end up on the internet somewhere!" Mason grinned down at her, an easy smile on an undeniably handsome—and arrogant—face. "And you think this is funny?"

"One thing you've got to know about firefighters is that we like to joke around. Our jobs are so intense, it's important to find ways to make it light." He shrugged his shoulders. "And, you did call me a caveman. I believe, from what I've learned about caveman, that they're prone to knocking woman over the head and taking them over their shoulders."

Sabrina turned away from him, her breathing erratic as she tried to calm herself. She was angry. But she was also turned on. Being in his arms like that, she'd felt a purely sensual reaction to him.

Two young women in their early twenties walked toward Sabrina and Mason en route to their own car. "Are you really a firefighter?" one of them asked, looking up at Mason's helmet.

"Yes, I am."

"Lucky you," the other one said to Sabrina, before remotely unlocking the car behind Sabrina's Equinox.

The two women then giggled as they got into their vehicle. Sabrina turned back toward Mason, leveling an angry stare in his direction. "You shouldn't have done that."

"It's my view that everyone can benefit from a little lighthearted goofing around. Maybe some more than others."

"Are you trying to say I'm uptight?"

"The only thing I know about you for sure is that you're a tough cookie. But I look forward to learning more about you at dinner. Unless you'd prefer we only go for a drink."

Sabrina marched toward her driver's-side door and opened it. "Mason, it was nice working with you. Now, I must be on my way."

She climbed into her car, slammed the door and quickly started the engine. She then she drove off, leaving Mason standing at the curb, looking after her.

Chapter 5

Of all the completely insane things for a man to do! The next morning, Sabrina was still livid. She couldn't believe that Mason had actually had the nerve to throw her over his shoulder in front of strangers at the beach. She was humiliated!

Who knew if photos of the embarrassing incident would end up on the internet? Or even video? She was a professional in Ocean City. She didn't need to have photos berating her reputation online.

But worse than what had happened was that Sabrina had a reaction to Mason's ridiculous behavior. A small part of her had actually felt a thrill. Sabrina still felt an odd tingle in her nether region when she thought about how Mason scooped her into his arms. He had picked her up as though she weighed no more than a rag doll. His strength was impressive and her attraction to him electric.

After that initial rush, reality had set in, and her embarrassment had taken over. Embarrassment and outrage.

As Sabrina had lain in bed not sleeping, she'd dreamed about what had happened earlier that day. Though her dream had gone in a completely different direction. Once Mason had put her down, he had kissed her senseless.

When Sabrina woke up, she was hardly rested—and it was all Mason's fault. As she got ready for her day, she thought about how nonroutine her photo shoot with Mason had been. Of all the shoots she had done in her career, his had been the most unusual.

Dressed and ready to work, Sabrina made her way downstairs. Although her studio and office were housed in the lower part of the house, she physically had to exit her apartment upstairs, go down the staircase in order to open her locked office. It was the best of both worlds. One, it was cheaper having her office and studio in the space where she lived. Two, having to physically exit her apartment and go downstairs was akin to getting in a car and heading to the office. Only this way, she didn't have to deal with the commute.

There was a small kitchen in her office, and she placed a pod of French Vanilla coffee into her instant brewing machine—truly the best invention since the toaster, in her opinion. A short while later, she was heading into her personal office with a steaming cup of java.

Sitting at her desk, she fired up her computer. The Apple computer had a twenty-seven inch screen, which was excellent for viewing several photos at once. She retrieved her camera and unloaded the SD card she had used to take the shots of Mason, then inserted it into her computer.

But instead of looking at photos of Mason, she opened the folder with the pictures of Ricardo, another firefighter. She needed to get Mason off of her mind, at least for a little while.

She heard Nya enter the office by the clicking of her heels on the tiled floor. Based on the quick succession of clicks, she could tell that Nya was moving around hurriedly. And she knew why. It was ten minutes after ten, meaning that Nya was late.

"Morning," Nya said, peeking her head through Sabrina's office door. "Sorry I'm late."

"It's all right," Sabrina told her. "Does that mean you had a great date?"

Nya rolled her eyes. "No. The date was a disaster."

"Oh, no."

"I mean, Sean started out great. He seemed really nice, a total gentleman…until we were at my car and he groped me and did his best to get me to go to bed with him."

Sabrina grimaced. "Oh, boy."

"He said he thought I'd be down for it. That I *looked* the type. I almost slapped him."

"Well," Sabrina began cautiously, "I've told you this before—maybe you should change your online profile. You've got some really sexy pictures up there—nothing inappropriate, mind you—but I think it gives *some* men the wrong idea."

"I think I'm finally done with dating. I can't take the stress anymore." Nya shook her head and made a sound of disgust. "How about you? How was yesterday with Mason?" She wiggled her eyebrows.

"It was a good shoot," Sabrina told her.

"And…?"

"And nothing."

"Nothing?"

"We left the studio, went to the beach. I got some incredible shots." Sabrina quickly brought her coffee mug to her lips, hoping that Nya wouldn't pick up on the fact that she was omitting a huge portion of the story.

"Bummer." Nya pouted.

"Because you expected us to make a love connection?"

"Well. Yeah. I totally saw a different you yesterday."

"He's a cute guy," Sabrina said, hoping that her acknowledgment of that would be enough for Nya.

Nya's pout lingered. "I'm going to go get some coffee and head to my desk. I swear, love sucks."

Nya left the office, and Sabrina went back to looking through the photos of Ricardo. She smiled, happy with what she had done. The photos looked incredible.

She looked over the pictures of the other firefighters, as well, before finally going over the hundreds of photos she had taken of Mason the day before. A part of her didn't want to do even that. She truly wished that she didn't have to see him again, not even in pictures.

The door to her office suddenly opened. Looking toward the door, Sabrina's eyes widened in alarm. The bouquet of dazzling red roses was so large that she couldn't even see who was carrying them. It was only when she heard Nya speak that she realized her friend was behind the flowers.

Nya placed the bouquet of what looked to be at least fifty red roses down on her desk with a huff. Nya then planted her hands on her hips. "You lied to me."

"What are you talking about?" Sabrina asked.

"You told me that nothing happened with you and Mason yesterday. That there was no spark. So explain this." Nya gestured to the impressive bouquet.

"Those are for me?"

Nya rolled her eyes. "Girl, if they were for me I would not have marched that heavy bouquet back here just to see the look on your face. Unless you're seeing someone else, my bet is that these are from Mason."

Sabrina reached for the card that was perched on a holder and quickly opened the envelope and read.

I want you to know that I'm not really a caveman. Sorry if I offended you by trying to have a little fun yesterday. It's just my nature. My offer of dinner still stands. That way you can get to know the real me. Mason

"Why didn't you tell me that you two hit it off?" Nya demanded. "Because obviously you did. A man doesn't send you an exquisite bouquet like this when you haven't hit it off."

Sabrina inhaled a deep breath. She had avoided telling Nya about yesterday, hoping she could put it out of her mind altogether. She was attracted to Mason, she had come to that conclusion. But she also knew that she wasn't the only woman who felt a pull of desire where the sexy firefighter was concerned.

And whatever attraction he felt toward her, which had inspired him to send these roses…was obviously based on the physical. Not that she had a problem with that. Attraction started that way. But Sabrina could already see the big picture with a man like Mason. She could already see the heartbreak down the road.

"Well?" Nya prompted.

"I wouldn't exactly say we had a connection."

Nya eyed Sabrina with suspicion. "Then why did he send you all of these roses?"

"I don't know. I guess—"

Before Sabrina could finish speaking, Nya snatched the card from Sabrina's hand.

"Hey!" Sabrina protested.

As Nya read, her eyes filled with excitement, then narrowed with question. "What does he mean about this caveman bit?"

"He acted like one," Sabrina responded, glad to finally be able to tell her friend what had transpired. "He actually grabbed me and threw me over his shoulder."

"What?"

"You heard me."

Nya squealed and did a little foot-stomping routine, as though that was the most exciting thing she had ever heard. "Get out!"

"I'm serious."

"Wow." Nya sat on the chair opposite Sabrina's desk and pulled it closer to her. "Tell me everything. From the moment you left here to when you got to the beach to when you guys parted. Because there are clearly a lot of pieces of this story that you need to fill in for me."

So Sabrina told her. Told her how the shoot had gone well, and how he had made some flirtatious comments, which easily could have been playful banter. "And then he asked me out. When I told him I wasn't interested, he assumed that I wasn't interested in men. Can you believe that?" Recalling that particular part had Sabrina's fire building again. "That's when I called him a Neanderthal. I think I mentioned the word *caveman* a couple of times. The next thing I knew he was throwing me over his shoulder to prove a point. God, I was so humiliated."

"That is undoubtedly the most action you have had in two years. And you were *humiliated?*"

Sabrina's face flushed. She had been embarrassed, yes, but she had also felt an irrational thrill. "Yes, I was humiliated. We were at a public beach."

"This is me you're talking to. And I saw Mason. Are you going to tell me that you weren't even the least bit turned on when that hunk of a man slung you over his shoulder?"

Sabrina's lips parted. She wanted to tell Nya that she was wrong, that she hadn't in the least been turned on. But that would be an outright lie.

Her silence was all the confirmation Nya needed. She squealed again. "Oh, my goodness. I love it!"

Sabrina rolled her eyes. "You would."

"And you *should.* Come on, a guy as hot as Mason is interested in you—"

"And how many other women? I wasn't born yesterday."

"Certainly you can go to dinner with him."

"Why?" Sabrina protested. "You know my stance on dating. I don't really want to go out with anyone until I feel a real connection. A soul connection. The kind of connection that will lead to forever."

"Which you can't possibly know the first time you meet someone. You have to give people a chance before you can see where it might go. That's why God created dating. You should totally go to dinner with Mason."

Sabrina shook her head. "With a guy like Mason, it's obvious what he's after. I'm not trying to be judgmental, but he's amazingly hot."

"You're selling yourself short. Just because Lester left you—"

"This isn't about that."

"Then what is it about? You've always had this attitude where you seem to believe you're not good enough."

"I have never said that."

"Not explicitly, no. But somewhere deep inside, that's what you feel. I know your father was a schmuck. I know Lester hurt you. And in college, Jackson—"

"Okay, you don't have to name all the men who have disappointed me in my life."

"I'm just telling you that you can let go of some of that. Take Mason's interest for what it is. A guy who wants to get to know you. Don't jump into it already thinking that it can't work without giving it the chance to."

Sabrina waved a dismissive hand. She didn't want to hear this from Nya. No matter how many bad relationships Nya had gotten into, she still had a sense of optimism about the next one.

"I think…I think that Mason was just reacting to the fact that we were alone together for quite some time yesterday. That's why he asked me out."

"Hogwash," Nya said. "It wasn't like you just spent three months alone together in Siberia, gimme a break."

"I don't think I'm his type."

"He met you, he was attracted to you and he wants to take you to dinner. And for the first time in two years

I've seen you actually show some emotion…*and you told him no?*"

"I'm working on the calendar," Sabrina stressed. "Mixing business with pleasure is not the smartest thing to do."

"No, I think it's a very smart thing to do. Kill two birds with one stone."

Sabrina made a face. "Two birds with one stone. You're funny."

"How often do you meet a man as gorgeous as Mason Foley? My goodness, girl, do you need to be hit over the head to know that you should go for it?"

"And end up with heartbreak?"

"Stop assuming that it won't work out."

Sabrina wished she could be more like Nya. Because the truth was, her curiosity about Mason had definitely been piqued. And now, seeing the flowers, her heart was suddenly fluttering with excitement.

Which she tried to suppress. No matter how much she was attracted to him. Dating men based on physical attraction in the past had led to heartbreak, and she wanted to spare herself the pain.

"You're really not going to call him?" Nya asked. "Not even to say thanks for the flowers?"

Sabrina shook her head. "I wasn't born yesterday. I rejected the guy, and now he's suddenly sending me a ridiculous amount of roses. Guys like Mason love to chase. They go for the kill. Then they get you, and before you know it, it's over."

"But think of the fun you could have along the journey. Before things ended with Jackson in college, I remember you telling me you were having the time of your life."

Just the mention of Jackson's name had Sabrina's chest tightening painfully. Yes, she had been married to Lester, but before that, Jackson was the one who had broken her heart. She had learned a valuable lesson about dating a guy that every woman wanted.

"Thank you for bringing up Jackson, because I learned that lesson once, and I am not about to be burned twice."

"Dinner. Come on, it can't kill you. And maybe even a little more than dinner. Honestly, two years to go without getting any…it's almost obscene."

"I'd prefer that to finding Mr. Right every other month, then calling your best friend in tears." Sabrina gave Nya a pointed look.

Nya's lips tightened, knowing the comment was meant for her. "At least I'm getting out there. I'm not afraid to put my heart on the line."

"Nya, I'm sorry. I didn't mean to sound harsh."

"Sure, you did. But you know what? You can't protect your heart by becoming a block of ice. It doesn't work that way."

"Nya…" But Nya was already walking out of Sabrina's office.

When Nya was gone, Sabrina buried her face in her hands and groaned. She hadn't meant to offend her friend, even if they did have different philosophies on the best way to find love. The problem was, Nya made it sound so easy, but Sabrina knew better.

Maybe Nya's right, Sabrina thought. *Maybe I should have said yes.*

Of course you should have said no! You can't go on a date with a guy like Mason Foley!

Nya wasn't the first person to say that she was cold. People had accused her of that before, although those who knew her also knew that she had a warm heart. But Nya's words were making her think about how things had transpired with Mason. And perhaps that her initial response to him had been a little…well, callous.

As quick and decisive as she had been, she had cut him

off at the knees, so to speak. They'd had a good photo shoot, had developed a good rapport, and perhaps Sabrina simply should have said yes to dinner to be polite. After all, didn't she want to be hired to do more calendars for the Fire Department in the future?

Her stomach sank. She hadn't been considering the big picture. She could have said yes to dinner, treated it as a business venture and kept things between them cordial and light. She should have been thinking about securing a relationship with the Ocean City Fire Department for years to come. Now, she could only hope that the events that had transpired didn't negatively affect her chances of being hired by the fire department in the future.

It was just that…well, she hadn't expected the offer of dinner. And God knew that the last thing she wanted was a distraction in her life right now in the form of a man. Business was picking up, and she far preferred the idea of wooing more jobs as opposed to wooing a man.

Sabrina's computer screen had gone black to sleep mode, and she looked at her reflection. As her eyes settled on her mouth, she thought about how it had been way too long since a man had kissed her.

Touched her.

There was no doubt that a man like Mason could perk up a woman's libido. But if all Sabrina wanted was sex, she could have had that a long time ago. No, what she hoped for—if the right man ever came around—was the total package. A man who would love her completely, and support her dreams.

And make wild, passionate love to her.

Even when she had been married to Lester, the sex hadn't been that phenomenal. But she'd loved him, and had planned to build a life with him. Lester, who had approached her on the pier when she'd had a camera in her hand, had known how much photography meant to her.

She didn't simply take pictures. Being a photographer is who she was.

So it had come as a huge shock when Lester had started complaining about the hours she kept, and had all but demanded that she cut back on the time that she spent doing what she loved. For a photographer who was finally making a name for herself, cutting down on business at the time would have been career-suicide. In an effort to please Lester, Sabrina had hired on another photographer at her studio, but Lester hadn't liked the guy. According to her husband, Floyd—who had been happily married—wanted to get into her pants.

Now that their marriage was over, Sabrina sometimes wondered if Lester had secretly wanted her business to fail. His brothers had wives who stayed at home, as his mother had done. Lester's job in construction had been secure, and he could have supported both of them, but what was Sabrina supposed to do? Even if she could imagine herself staying at home until her children went to school, what would she do after that? Take up knitting? Join a group that met once a week at the library? Learn how to bake even though she was a disaster in the kitchen? God bless those whose passion was as a homemaker. But being a stay-at-home mother and wife would have killed her, surely.

She pressed her mouse to bring the screen to life, wondering why she had even started thinking of Lester and marriage. All because Mason had asked her on a date?

And there he was, on her screen. The current photo was of him standing on the beach, his back to the water, his face turned to the side as if he were looking off at a fire in the distance. He was shirtless, his suspenders over his shoulders, his helmet on his head, and an axe in his hands.

The man was too fine.

And Sabrina suddenly understood why she had pushed him away so quickly. Because the truth was, she knew that she could easily throw all of her morals out the window and jump into bed with him.

She laughed at how quickly she had jumped from *A* to *Z* without any reason to. Mason hadn't even asked her out on a date, really. He had simply invited her to dinner. And probably just to be nice.

She wondered what information there was about him on the web. Moments later, she found herself opening up a search engine on the internet and typing in Mason's name.

It didn't take long for a list of results to pop up. And one of the links shocked her.

Mason Foley Inks Eight-Figure NBA Deal.

Sabrina's eyes bulged. She scanned the other hits under his name, certain this was a different Mason Foley than the one who lived in Ocean City. There were more articles surrounding basketball, convincing her that Mason Foley the Fire Captain could not be the same man mentioned in these articles.

But since articles pertaining to basketball were the majority of the results she found, she clicked on one of the links.

Her lips parted in surprise when she saw Mason's photo.

It was undoubtedly him. A younger him. The date of the article had been sixteen years ago. In the photo accompanying the story, Mason had dreadlocks, but that same, charming smile made it clear that he was the same man she had met.

Mason Foley firefighter had once been Mason Foley NBA star.

She read article after article, learning of his great promise in the NBA. How he had been a first round draft pick with a dream contract at the age of twenty. But apparently after his five-year contract had been up, he'd decided to walk away from the sport. A move that had shocked industry experts and fans alike. But what had convinced some die-hard sports analysts that Mason had lost his mind was the fact that he'd gone into firefighting.

Mason's statement remained consistent when asked about his controversial decision. He claimed a desire to truly give back to his community is what led him to firefighting.

"What?" Sabrina asked aloud, frowning. Like everyone else who had been puzzled by Mason's decision, she didn't understand it, either. She didn't know anyone who would walk away from a huge career in sports to pursue public service.

Sabrina leaned back in her chair and narrowed her eyes as she looked at the computer screen, suddenly much more curious about Mason Foley.

Chapter 6

As the Ocean City pier came into view, Mason sped up for the last hundred yards of his five-mile run. A burst of adrenaline helped him to push through to the end point, beating his friend Tyler in the final dash to their pre-determined finish line.

Behind him, Mason heard Tyler grunting frustration. "Damn it, not again!"

Bending over to catch his breath, Mason faced his friend and grinned. "You've got to step it up, my man."

Tyler came to a stop beside him and after inhaling several deep breaths, began to pace. "I have been stepping it up. It's those long legs of yours. You have an unfair advantage."

"Excuses, excuses," Mason said. Though in reality, he knew that Tyler was right. At six foot two, Tyler was definitely a tall guy. But Mason towered over most men.

Mason took the water bottle from the fuel belt around his waist, opened it and drank almost all of the contents in one long gulp. He saw that Tyler was doing the same thing.

Mason checked the stopwatch in his hand, which he had clicked as he had crossed the finish line. Then said, "At least our time is better. We shaved off a good two minutes from the last time we came out here."

"Impressive." Tyler had his hand on one side as he continued to catch his breath.

The two of them were training for a marathon coming

up in four months, the Run for the Cure. Tyler's mother had died of breast cancer just last year, so doing this run was important to him. And all of the firefighters at nearby Station Four had been touched by cancer when Ronald McIntire, a fellow firefighter, had been diagnosed with prostate cancer at the age of thirty-eight. He was in remission now, but the reality that cancer often hit men in the field of firefighting was something neither of them could ignore. So Mason was happy to do whatever he could to help raise money to find a cure to finally rid the world of the deadly disease.

"Yeah, we got this," Mason said, and then slapped hands with Tyler. "Come August, if we don't come first and second…"

"Me first, you second," Tyler said.

"Yeah, right."

Tyler glanced upward, and then pointed a finger in the same direction. "As long as I do this for my mother, that's all that matters. I can't help her, but I know she would want me to do this. I can't wait until the day that we can finally kick cancer's butt."

"You can say that again."

Mason wandered to the edge of the pier, cordoned off with concrete and a rope chain. He looked out at the boats sailing and thought of his own mother. How he had lost her far too soon.

"I heard from Sully today," Tyler began, coming to stand beside him. "That fire was definitely arson. These restaurant owners also complained of threats, just like the first case last week. So, what is this? Someone with a vendetta against restaurants?"

"Damn." Mason gritted his teeth. That was the last thing they needed. Having to deal with an arsonist who might strike again at anytime? That reality could make for several tense nights until the arsonist was caught.

Mason's gaze wandered back to the Pacific. Just yesterday, he had been out along this beachfront with Sabrina, albeit ten miles north. She had consumed his thoughts all night, despite her rejection.

By now, she must have received his flowers. He had hoped that she would call him, express thanks. But thus far, she hadn't.

Flowers were a more traditional touch. He hoped that the note he'd sent would bring a smile to her face, and show her that he indeed wasn't a caveman.

But he was starting to wonder why she hadn't yet called him. Because even though she had rejected him, he hadn't seen it as that. She had gotten all uptight after he had suggested they go to dinner, and he figured it was because she was the type who didn't like to mix business with pleasure. She had made that point clear. What he hoped was that she was intrigued enough by him that she would break her rule.

After all, it wasn't like he'd proposed marriage. He simply wanted to spend more time with her.

Mason wasn't used to hearing no, and perhaps that interested him all the more. He actually appreciated the chase. All too often, some women said yes too easily. Or worse, they went after him without abandon. At thirty-five years old, he was the kind of guy who enjoyed pursuing a woman. Maybe he was too traditional, but he felt it was the man's role to do the serious courting.

Which was the reason he had sent Sabrina the flowers. If she didn't respond to that, he would send her something else. Maybe chocolates. He would continue until she said yes to dinner.

"Hey," Tyler suddenly said, "you didn't tell me how the photo shoot went yesterday."

Mason faced him. "It was great. Easy as pie."

"You're a natural, huh?"

"Some of us got it like that," Mason teased.

"Then it should be a breeze for me," Tyler said. "I go on Friday."

"You'll like Sabrina. She's very smart. When it comes to photos, she knows her stuff. I was impressed. And she's beautiful. Real easy on the eyes."

Tyler flashed him an odd look. "Beautiful?"

"Yeah. Not in that in-your-face kind of way. It's more understated." Something Mason totally appreciated. He typically met the kind of women who took an hour to put on their makeup, then another hour to decide on the perfect outfit. He actually preferred a woman who was comfortable in sweats and no makeup, but could also dress to the nines when the occasion required.

Tyler's eyes narrowed as Mason's cell phone rang. He reached for it expectantly, pulling it from the grip around his waist. But when he saw the number, he decided not to answer.

"You not answering your phone?" Tyler asked.

"Nope."

"Who was it?"

"Kenya."

Now Tyler's expression turned to stunned. "And you didn't pick up?"

Mason merely shrugged. "I'll talk to her later."

Tyler continued to look at him as though he had been replaced with a stranger. "You'll talk to Kenya later? Kenya the model, the one with legs for days? Not to mention the rest of ..."

"Yep, that's the one," Mason interrupted.

"Maybe something happened to you during the run. Maybe too much oxygen drained from your head or something. I think we should head to the station and have one of the EMTs check you out."

"Like I said, I'll talk to her later."

Mason began walking toward where he'd parked his

car, and Tyler fell into step beside him. "You were hot for Kenya," he pressed on. "Then she went off to Europe, isn't she just getting back? For weeks all you could talk about was that you were counting the days until she returned. Now she's back and you don't want to pick up?"

Mason knew that Tyler wasn't going to stop asking questions. His friends at the firehouse had practically lost their marbles when Kenya had shown up at the station the first time. She had been decked out in a strapless dress that hugged her large breasts and flowed over her narrow waist, and stopped midthigh. The five-inch wedge heels on her feet only helped to make her slim legs look even longer. There was no doubt about it, she was a knockout.

Her body was a perfect ten, and she knew how to flaunt it. When Mason had gone out with her, people had stopped and turned heads to stare. It had done wonders for his ego to know that he was with a woman whom his friends and other men desired.

The first month that she was gone, he had even missed her. And then he'd wondered what exactly he was missing. Because the more he'd gotten to know Kenya, the more he'd realized that she wasn't the kind of woman you could talk to. She didn't even keep abreast of current affairs. The month after they'd gotten involved, a six-year-old girl had been abducted in Ocean City. When Mason had brought up the distressing situation with Kenya, she hadn't even known what he was talking about, and blamed it on the fact that she didn't watch or read the news.

Kenya's interests were shopping, celebrity news and gossip. Lord knew she could talk forever about what she'd bought in Paris, and the perfect outfit she'd picked up in Milan. None of that interested Mason.

Their relationship had been physical, plain and simple. Initially Mason had hope that they could develop to be more than that, but they had never truly developed an emotional bond.

"I've kind of gotten bored of her," Mason said with a shrug.

"What?" Tyler looked dumbfounded. "With a girl like that? Women as beautiful as her don't come around too often. No, make that ever."

"She's beautiful, yes. But there's more to life than beauty."

Tyler clutched his chest, as though he was suddenly hit with searing heart spasms. "I don't believe what I just heard. Seriously, bro, I'm starting to think you're not okay. Maybe it's time for you to stop training so hard for this marathon."

"I asked out Sabrina," Mason finally said, tired of hearing Tyler go on about Kenya. "The photographer. I suggested dinner. I don't know…I kind of felt that there was something between us yesterday. So…"

Several beats passed as Tyler stared at him, both of his eyebrows rising with curiosity. "You like the photographer? Well, damn. Why didn't you say so?"

"Because I just met her yesterday. I figured I'd go to dinner with her first before telling you about it."

Tyler shook his head, a grin of admiration on his lips. "Dang, Mason. When I grow up, I want to be as smooth as you."

Mason chuckled. "You've already got Carol."

"Now I can't wait to see this woman. When are you going out?"

"Actually." Mason frowned slightly. "She turned down my offer of dinner."

Tyler slapped him on the back and laughed. "You're kidding?"

"For now," Mason stressed.

"A woman who rejected you," Tyler said with awe.

"Not every woman is easy. And actually, it's refreshing."

"Is that what you call it?"

"Sure. Where's the challenge when a woman says yes immediately? When I met Kenya, she was all over me instantly. And then she expected me to take her to all of the most high-end places. Now don't get me wrong, I enjoy treating a woman right. But I don't enjoy when it seems that the only thing a woman wants from you is your wallet."

Tyler eyed him skeptically, and then asked, "So what is it about this photographer that has you forgetting about Kenya?"

"For one thing, not only is she beautiful, she's also smart. Clearly driven. I don't know. There was just something about her that intrigued me. I definitely felt a connection, and it wasn't a connection based on her knowing about my past in basketball." When Mason had met Kenya, she had known immediately who he was. "I'd like to get to know her better. See where things go."

"All right. Well at least I know you're not dead. Because for a minute I was beginning to wonder."

"I sent her flowers today. And reiterated my offer of dinner."

"And?"

"And I haven't heard from her yet."

"Maybe you're losing your touch. Maybe whatever charisma you had went to Europe with Kenya."

"Oh, I'll hear from her. Eventually."

"I am definitely interested in meeting this woman who has pulled you out of the Kenya clouds. Because confession time—as beautiful as Kenya is, I didn't really like her that much."

"Now you tell me."

"She's gorgeous, yes—and I got why you were into her—but she always seemed shallow."

"You picked up on that from the few times you met her?"

"Yeah. Nice girl, just...not much substance."

Mason was glad to hear his friend say that, because those were his feeling exactly. Kenya was great to hang out with, but long-term? She wasn't right for him.

But Sabrina... Time would tell if there was any potential for them.

Chapter 7

Friday, Sabrina was looking forward to the next session with the firefighter she would photograph. His name was Tyler McKenzie, and like Mason he had classically good looks. His cheeks were more chiseled, his nose straighter and his skin lighter. From the snapshots she'd seen of him when she'd first scouted potential models from the firehouses, Tyler appeared to be fairly photogenic, as well. He'd been with the fire service for fourteen years, and worked as an engineer at the station. Given that, Sabrina figured it'd be great to take at least some photos of him alongside the fire engine he commanded.

But first, he was coming to the studio so that she could capture some shots of him. From here, they could head back to the station, which wasn't far, to get the remaining shots she needed.

When Nya walked into the studio, Sabrina gave her a once-over. Nya was all decked out in four-inch patent beige pumps and a colorful minidress. She had a chunky necklace around her neck with the same reds, purples and pinks in her dress. On her left wrist, she had an array of sparkly bangles in similar colors. Her hair was softly curled, and her makeup applied perfectly.

"Hot date after work?" Sabrina asked.

"Another firefighter is coming in today," Nya said. "If he looks anything like Mason, I want to be prepared."

"I should have known." Sabrina rolled her eyes.

"Girl, you know every woman loves a man in uniform. Speaking of which, have you called Mason?"

"Nope."

Nya said nothing more on the subject. Obviously after their conversation on Wednesday, Nya had figured it was best not to push the issue.

Three hours later, when Tyler came into her office, Sabrina was at the front talking with Nya about a cancellation. The door opened, and in he walked, greeting both of them with an instant and bright smile.

"Oh, hello." Nya quickly scooted around from behind the desk and offered him her hand. "You must be Tyler McKenzie." She grinned, and Sabrina witnessed the not-so-subtle way Nya's eyes focused on his wedding hand. "My name is Nya, and I am Sabrina's assistant-office manager. Anything you need, just ask, and I'll get it for you."

Sabrina walked toward Tyler. "Hello, Tyler. I'm Sabrina. Pleasure to meet you."

He looked at her with an odd smile on his face. It was the kind of smile that made Sabrina wonder if she had something caught in her teeth.

His look of amusement intensified, which made Sabrina feel a little anxious.

"So you're Sabrina," Tyler said, his voice a little sing-songish.

Sabrina was confused. "Yes, that's me."

"I've heard a lot about you."

"Good things, I hope?"

"Definitely. Mason Foley, whom you photographed a few days ago, speaks very highly of you."

Sabrina's heart accelerated at his statement, but she tried not to show that she'd been affected by Tyler's words. Since receiving the flowers, she hadn't called Mason, and she hadn't heard from him.

"Really?" Sabrina asked. And then, "I'm glad he enjoyed the session."

Again, Tyler gave her a look that seemed to have a secret meaning. And it dawned on her that Mason must have told him that he had asked her out. But she wasn't about to get into that with him. Instead, she gestured toward the hallway that leads to the studio. "The studio's down there. If you can bring your bag down with you, we can discuss the shot that I'd like to take. But first, would you like a coffee, or a tea? Water?"

"No, I'm fine."

Nya approached him. "Are you sure? I'm here to help. By the way, I just love firefighters. You all risk your lives to keep us safe, and the least I can do is make you a coffee or tea ór even offer you one of these luscious pastries we get from a shop across the street. If you've never been to Sweet Treats, you really should try it. It's—"

"Nya," Sabrina said, her tone holding a warning. "He's fine. But why don't you check in on us in twenty minutes or so?"

Tyler nodded. "Yeah, that would be good."

"In fact, why don't you go and pick up a half dozen of Jean's cupcakes?" After three photography sessions, the treats Nya had picked up that morning were finished.

"Will do," Nya said.

Sabrina led Tyler into her studio, where she discussed with him the ideas she had for the shoot. "And as I said to you when we spoke, I'd really love to get some shots of you in front of your fire engine, so once we're finished here, if you don't mind going over to the station that would be great."

"That's fine by me."

They spent an hour in her studio, getting a variety of shots. Just like Mason, Tyler was a natural.

It was just before five when Nya came into the studio,

offering Tyler a snack and drink. Almost begging him to have something. "I'm going to be heading out soon, so it's now or never," she said sweetly. "And you really should try one of the cupcakes. Before I eat another one and add even more inches to my hips."

"Looks like a few inches wouldn't hurt you any," Tyler said.

"No?" Nya asked, and actually batted her eyelashes.

"Definitely not. You've got a beautiful shape."

She blushed. "Why thank you."

"I love a woman with a figure. I tell my fiancée all the time that I like her just the way she is."

Sabrina saw the light in Nya's eyes fizzle out. "Oh." It took her a moment to regain her composure. "Well, aren't you a wonderful fiancé."

"I'll have a coffee, black. And one of those cupcakes. Since you say they're awesome."

"Sure."

As Nya left the studio, Sabrina couldn't help smirking a little. Even if she did feel a smidgen sorry for her friend. So much for blind optimism. Maybe Nya would realize once and for all that finding love wasn't as easy as flirting and going out on dates.

Heck, if it were that easy, would anyone be single?

The following Tuesday, Chief Tom Sully was due to come into Sabrina's office for a meeting regarding how the calendar was coming along. Sabrina was extremely pleased. She only had two more firemen to photograph, and was elated with the results so far. The photos were artistic and sexy, and she was certain that the calendar would be a huge hit.

It was just after one-thirty when Nya came into Sabrina's office. "Hey," she said. "I'm gonna get out of here so that I make it to my dentist's appointment for two."

."No problem."

"I made all the calls you asked me to, and confirmed every appointment. And I left a message for Tom Sully that I won't be here when he arrives, so if you're not at the front he should just go on back to your office."

"That's great. Thanks." Sometimes Sabrina forgot about time while she was working. She was currently going through the photos from a wedding before the recently returned honeymooners came into the office later that day to see the pictures.

"Talk to you later," Nya said.

"Yep."

Sabrina spent fifteen more minutes selecting through photos of the wedding that she believed were best before opening up the folder that held all of the pictures she had taken of the firefighters. That main folder was broken down into subfolders for each firefighter, and also a subfolder of the pictures that she believed were the best. This meeting with Tom was to show him her progress so far, and to see if he had any drastic ideas about how to do things differently.

Sabrina was just hanging up the phone with a potential client when she heard the knock on her office door. "Come in," she called.

She looked in the direction of the door as it opened, Sabrina got to her feet and smiled, ready to greet Tom Sully. But her smile went flat when saw the person who actually entered her office.

Mason Foley.

Sabrina jerked backward in surprise, a breath oozing out of her.

"I guess you weren't planning to call me back, after all." Smiling easily, Mason sauntered into the office.

"M-Mason," Sabrina stuttered. Her brain was going

blank as her eyes focused on the extremely sexy man whose presence filled her office.

"You kept the flowers at least," he said. "That's a good sign."

"This is really not the best time," Sabrina said, recovering her ability to speak. "I'm expecting Tom Sully any moment so that we can go over the photos for the calendar."

Mason continued walking toward her, and Sabrina had to resist the urge to step backward. "Then you're in luck," Mason told her. "Because I'm now the go-to man for everything pertaining to the calendar."

Sabrina's eyes widened. She could hardly breathe, much less to speak.

"I talked to Tom, and he agreed that it would be best if I took over," Mason explained.

Sabrina's eyes finally narrowed. "Why? Why would you insert yourself into my dealings with Tom?"

"It was one way to see you again."

Sabrina was infuriated. "This business with the calendar…I take it very seriously. I don't know what kind of game you're playing, but I don't like it."

"And you have no reason to worry. Because I'm here for business. In fact, Tom trusts me completely. He feels that I'm probably better suited to make these decisions, anyway. He said he can hardly tell the difference between a cartoon picture and digital print." Mason paused, as though hoping Sabrina would crack a smile. "I took an advertising class in college, plus I have an appreciation for photography."

What kind of photography? Posters of half-naked women he could hang on a wall?

"Ultimately, we'll be deferring to your expertise," Mason went on. "Rest assured, I'm here to work. Naturally, the calendar's outcome is of paramount importance to the fire station."

Sabrina drew in a few deep breaths to calm herself.

Okay, so Mason was here instead of Tom. He said he was here for business, so she would do with him what she had planned to do with Tom.

"Okay. If you're here to work, then this seat's for you." She patted the leather chair beside her.

Mason sank into the chair and turned his attention to the computer screen. Sabrina opened up the folder with the photos she felt were the strongest for use in the calendar.

"These are the ones I really like, and I'm having trouble deciding between a few of them, so maybe you can help me narrow them down. After all, it is a calendar for the firefighters so your input will be valuable."

They spent quite a bit of time going over the numerous shots. And to make things even more confusing, Sabrina decided to show him some of the other photos that were possibilities, which she had put into a different folder.

"It's all so much," Mason said.

"I know, it's a lot to choose from. I took so many photos. But you never know when you're going to get that perfect shot. Like that one of Carlos, right?"

"Yeah, that was a great shot." Sometimes, one shot was simply perfect and you knew it instantly. Upon seeing the one in question, Mason had agreed that the shot of Carlos in front of the ladder truck was spectacular.

"Which pictures of you yourself do you like the best?" Sabrina asked him. Had it been Tom here, she would have stuck with the photos of Mason she believed were the strongest. But she might as well get his opinion seeing that he was here.

Mason looked at the twenty pictures she had narrowed down for him. Each was vastly different. "I like the one with the backdrop of the flames in the studio." He shrugged. "Or this one on the beach," he said, pointing. "I love the way the rock formation looks behind me. And I also like the one with the cityscape behind me." He shook his head. "Honestly, I'm not sure which one is best. And I'm not sure I can be objective where I'm concerned. I'll leave the decision about which photo of me is best to you."

Sabrina pursed her lips. She wasn't sure which one was *the* perfect shot. There were so many amazing ones to choose from. Maybe she could use one shot of him for the front cover, and another shot of him inside the calendar.

She would decide that later, after playing around with the idea some more. She could also get a mockup calendar done with a few options so that she could visually see what she liked best. Then they could go from there.

"Well, I think that's it for now," Sabrina said. "We've narrowed down most of the shots, and the next thing will be to have a mock calendar made. You can discuss with the guys at the firehouse if they care which month they're featured. In the meantime, I will decide what I think is best. It will depend on how each works with the season." She shrugged, hoping for an indication whether or not he agreed.

"Sounds good to me."

"When would you like to see a mockup?"

"How fast can one be done?"

"I don't particularly want to rush it, but I'm sure one can be done in two weeks that I'll be happy with. We can make an appointment for you to come back and then go over—"

"I'm not sure I want to go another two weeks without seeing you."

Sabrina looked at Mason, whose eyes had taken on a different quality—one she wasn't comfortable with.

She pushed her chair back. "I'll be in touch—"

Mason gripped the armrest of her chair, preventing her from moving back farther. "Where are you running off to?"

"Our business is complete for today."

"That's right. The business is complete. Now we can concentrate on the personal."

Sabrina swallowed as a rush of heat washed over her.

Mason pulled her chair closer, his gaze holding hers.

"Mason." Sabrina made a sound of derision. "This is a little juvenile, don't you think? Trapping me like this?"

Mason released the chair. "You're free to stand up."

"Thank you." Sabrina quickly got up from her chair and headed for the office door, hoping that Mason would take that as his cue to leave.

"We can do this cat-and-mouse thing all day."

Now at the office door, Sabrina turned around. "You think I'm playing some sort of game?"

"Don't get me wrong, I'm totally up for the challenge."

"Challenge?" Sabrina shook her head. "Of course, that makes total sense. I already told you once, I'm not interested. And now that our business is over, I would like you to leave."

"Are you sure about that?"

"Of—of cou—" Why could she hardly speak?

Slowly, Mason walked toward her, his eyes locked on hers as though they were heat-seeking missiles. Sabrina's breath stopped. Instead of heading toward the open door, he moved toward where she stood at the wall beside the door. He didn't come to a stop until he was directly in front of her.

"What are you afraid of?" he asked as he looked down at her with his beguiling eyes.

"I—I'm not afraid of anything. I just—I have things to do."

Mason's lips curled in a slight smile. "So you *don't* want me to leave? You're just busy?"

"Mason…"

"I love it when you say my name. And when I look down at you…damn, you are so tempting. I just want to…"

His words trailed off as he brought a finger to her jaw-line and gently caressed it. Sabrina's body trembled in response.

"Yes." The word from his lips sounded almost like a sensuous sigh. "I knew that what I felt between us before was not imagined." His finger went to the other side of her face. "You feel something when I touch you."

There was a part of her that wanted to close her eyes and revel in the sensations his soft touch elicited. But the other part of her—the barrier she had put up to protect herself—remained intact.

"Mason, I don't understand what you're trying to prove."

He cocked his head to the side a little bit and placed one arm around her and against the wall, as though he intended to trap her there. "No?"

Sabrina looked up at him and saw him lick his lips. And then she watched with a sense of horror, disbelief and lust as his head began to lower. His eyes never leaving hers. Until finally, his lips came down, capturing her mouth.

And Lord help her, that first touch of his lips on hers was like she had touched a live wire. She felt a jolt of electricity shoot through her body. It was as though a part of her had been shocked back to life.

Her heart pounded out of control as Mason began to move his lips over hers with tantalizing slowness. Sweet heat spread through her.

And it felt so good.

Sabrina let herself surrender to this gorgeous man. Because there was just something thrilling about being chased.

But then thoughts filled her brain that jarred her from the moment. Cat and mouse. A game. This wasn't real, just something for Mason to entertain himself with.

Her lust subsiding, Sabrina broke the kiss and pushed him away from her, then quickly stepped past him.

She breathed in and out heavily, catching her breath and regaining her sanity. Why had she allowed him to kiss her like that?

"Why did you do that?" she demanded. "And after I told you to leave."

"Are you saying you didn't like it?"

"You can't just go around kissing people! There are laws against that!"

Mason flashed her an easy smile. "If I'm guilty of liking you, then I'll do the time."

Sabrina gaped at him. Did nothing faze him?

"I've said it before, and my feelings haven't changed. I definitely want to get to know you better."

Sabrina was flustered. He had an easy answer for everything. Of course he did. He had probably bed all kinds of women. For him, it was easy. His repertoire down. Heck, for all she knew, he had a playbook on how to handle various women. How to melt the resolve of every woman.

Turning away from him, she walked through her office door and to the front reception area. She paused only to open the front door and step outside. The air washed over her, and she gulped it in. The cool air had the effect of a slap in the face, sobering her.

She heard when Mason came out, and looked over her shoulder as he came to stand beside her. Then she looked out at the road.

"You, me, a couple of drinks, a nice meal…is it really so awful?"

Sabrina found the courage to face him. It wasn't that it was awful. Far from it. It would be nice to be like Nya and go out on a date with an attractive man.

Of course that was appealing.

The problem was what the next day would bring.

It wasn't that Sabrina didn't believe that Mason was into her. That was no longer a doubt. But the Masons of

the world were turned on by the chase more than anything. Once she said yes, he would lose interest. And that
would be that.

"Again, I appreciate your interest, but mostly I appreciate your business. And there's one thing I don't believe
in doing—and that's mixing business and pleasure. I do
apologize if I was too curt with you last week. I didn't
mean to come off as offensive. But today, I'm asking for
you to please respect my wishes. The last thing I need is
to get involved with you when I'm working on this calendar and have my integrity called into question. Other
photographers in the city might think I slept my way into
getting the job. And I don't want that to be the suspicion."

"That's what you're afraid of?"

Sabrina nodded, though she wasn't being entirely truth-
ful. "Yes. Please, let me concentrate on the work at hand.
That's what I need from you."

"Business." Mason seemed to mutter the word to himself, as though the concept was foreign to him. "All right.
I get it."

And then he turned and started toward his car, and Sabrina was a little surprised that the fight had gone out of
him so quickly. In fact, there was a small part of her that
was disappointed. Because the truth was, she had enjoyed
his kiss. For a few glorious seconds, she had felt completely alive.

Mason reached his car, and then stopped. Whirling
around, he began walking swiftly toward her, and alarm
shot through her body.

"What if I step down from my post as liaison for the
calendar?" he asked.

"Mason, that's not necessary."

"Because you don't plan to go out with me, right? Not
now, not ever."

Why was he making an issue out of this?

"It's not about business, is it?"

Sabrina blew out a huff of air and folded her arms over her chest. "I was trying to let you down easy."

"Let me down easy?" Mason threw his head back and laughed. "Listen, I'm not trying to force you to do anything. If you're not interested, just say it."

"Okay. I'm not… I'm just…" Why couldn't she say the words?

Mason's lips curled in a slow grin. "You can't even say it."

"You're not my type," she finally managed.

"Which isn't quite the same thing as saying that you're not interested?"

Sabrina swallowed. "You are incorrigible!"

"Is that a step up from caveman?"

"Why am I even out here having this conversation? I have work to do."

She turned.

"I think it's because no matter what you say to me, you know how you reacted when I kissed you. You liked it. A lot."

Sabrina opened the door to her office.

"Shall I make the dinner reservations? Saturday night will work for me."

Sabrina faced him. "I didn't say yes."

"I'll just keep sending flowers, chocolates, teddy bears—whatever it takes for you to say yes."

"Clearly you have money to burn. Do what you want."

Sabrina pulled the door open, and then stepped into her office. She gasped when Mason followed her back inside. And before she could utter a protest, he pulled her into his arms.

"Damn it, Sabrina," he said, his breath hot on her cheek. "Do you think it's my style to beg? God only knows why

I won't walk away from you with what you've told me, but...the way you kissed me says something different."

And as he held her in his arms and she looked up into his dark eyes, Sabrina wanted nothing more than for him to kiss her again.

Then he did. Sabrina balled her hands into fists and placed them against his chest. Not in protest, but because she didn't want to comply with what her body was telling her to do, which was snake her arms around his neck.

The kiss was slow and deep and oh, so hot. It was the kind of kiss that made Sabrina forget she was in her office, or even that the rest of the world existed. And just when she totally surrendered and gripped his shoulders, Mason eased back.

"That's why I don't want to take no for an answer," he told her. "Because of what I just felt when I kissed you. I have been rejected before, and I can tell you it *never* felt like that."

Sabrina was speechless. There was nothing she could say to dispute the truth. She was obviously madly attracted to Mason.

He took a step away from her, his eyes holding her gaze as he did. And as he edged closer to the door, Sabrina thought that he would say something. Anything.

Instead, he opened the door and slipped outside without saying another word to her.

Leaving Sabrina standing in her reception area feeling hot and bothered.

Chapter 8

Sabrina heard the door chimes for her office and knew that someone had entered. It was five-thirty, and Nya had left for the day half an hour ago.

"Hello?" she called, figuring Nya had forgotten to hang the CLOSED sign and that someone had wandered in.

Hearing no response, Sabrina headed out of her back office. And stopped in her tracks when she saw Mason standing there.

"M-Mason," she stuttered. "What are you doing back here?"

"You know why I'm here," he said, his voice sultry and his eyes dark with desire.

He began to walk toward her, slowly pulling his t-shirt over his head as he did. Sabrina's eyes bulged. But then her mouth started to water when he undid the clasp on his jeans.

"You know we both want this," he said as he came to stand in front of her. And then, wasting no time, he pulled her into his arms and kissed her.

His tongue was warm as it moved over hers urgently. His hands smoothed down her back until he gripped her behind. He pulled her against him, and she could feel his arousal, hard and firm.

"Say that you want me," Mason rasped. "I need to hear you say the words."

Sabrina looked up into Mason's handsome face and

knew that she wanted nothing more than to be with him. "I want you. I need you so badly."

With a groan of satisfaction, Mason kissed her again. And as he did, his hands slipped beneath her shirt. They felt warm against her skin as they moved upward. His fingers found her nipples and played with them, eliciting explosive pleasure.

"I am going to do things to you tonight that Lester never did. Nor Jackson. I'm going to make you forget about every man who has ever hurt you."

Even amid her pleasure, Sabrina felt slightly confused. "How do you know about Lester and Jackson?" she asked.

Mason didn't answer, just pushed her shirt out of the way, lowered his head and took a nipple into his mouth. The sensations were all encompassing, and she gripped his shoulders and held on as she rode the wave of bliss.

But she found herself wondering again how he knew about her ex-husband and her ex-boyfriend. And suddenly, her eyes flew open.

For a moment, Sabrina was disoriented. Her body was throbbing, and she didn't understand what was going on. Where was Mason?

It took her another moment to realize that she was in her bed. Alone.

Not downstairs in her studio. And Mason wasn't with her, seducing her.

She had been dreaming.

Her disappointment was profound. Five days had passed since she'd last seen him. He hadn't called. He hadn't texted. Hadn't dropped by.

And she actually missed him. She missed his playfulness and his bold flirtation.

Her body still tingling from the pleasurable dream, Sabrina got out of bed and began to get ready for work. She had a busy day ahead of her, with a wedding at City Hall, followed by photos with a couple at the beach. In the afternoon, she was going to be photographing a baby that was only a week old.

Her morning went by fast, and Sabrina stopped to grab a quick bite to eat after wrapping up the photo session with the newlyweds. She had just taken a bite of her pita when her cell phone rang. She stuck her hand in her bag and grabbed her phone, swiped across the screen to answer it and then put it to her ear. "Sabrina Crawford."

"I haven't heard from you," said the voice on the other end of the line.

Sabrina's pulse stumbled. "Mason?"

"You really know how to keep a guy waiting."

The edges of Sabrina's lips formed a smile. She was happy to hear his voice. Which surely made her crazy. Although she supposed the fact that he was giving her his attention did something for her ego, even if she didn't want to acknowledge it on a conscious level.

"If you're calling about the mockup calendar," she began, "it's not ready yet."

"Business, business," Mason said.

"I know I made myself clear," she said, not sure why she was continuing to pretend that she wasn't interested. In the five days since she hadn't heard from him, she had thought of him nonstop and wondered if it would be so bad to explore something with Mason—even if it were only physical. As Nya had said, it had been an obscenely long time since she'd had any action.

"And that's why I'm calling," Mason said. "Because of business."

"Oh." Her mood fizzled a little. "Good. I expect the mockup next week."

"That's great. The guys can't wait to see it."

"Would you like me to bring it to the station when it's ready? Of course, I'll call you first, set up a time."

"Sure. That'll work."

"Excellent. I'll call you next week, then."

"Always trying to get rid of me," Mason said before she could hang up. "You're gonna give me a complex."

"Actually, I'm just trying to eat a quick lunch before an appointment."

"Then I won't keep you. I wasn't calling about the calendar. I was actually hoping that I could hire you for something else."

"Hire me?" Sabrina asked, skeptical.

"Yeah. I'm going to a local burn unit on Sunday. I've started a charity to benefit the children's ward there. I plan to go with stuffed animals and other toys for the kids. I was planning to go solo, but if you could come along and get some photos of me and the kids, that would be great. I can put them up on the website."

Mason had started a charity? Sabrina was impressed. "You're serious?" she managed to say after a moment had passed.

"What—you think this is a ploy so I can see you again?"

Sabrina said nothing, but that was exactly what she'd been thinking.

"Yes, I'm serious," Mason went on when she didn't speak. "I wouldn't lie about this cause."

"You actually started a charity?"

"Uh-huh. Six months ago. A lot of firefighters support the burn center in many ways, but I wanted to take it one step further by founding a charity. Cancer charities and other ones get a ton of funding, but people don't think about burn victims. And burn victims' lives are often scarred forever. I'm not just talking about a burn on the skin. Some children are so badly injured in a fire that they have to learn how to walk again. The center does amazing work, but they're not the first charity people think of donating to. I'm hoping to change that."

Now Sabrina felt stupid for misjudging him. "Wow. That was a truly wonderful thing to do. What's the name of the charity?"

"The Miriam Foley Foundation. I named it after my mother. So, what do you say? Will you come and take some photos?"

"I'd be honored."

"Great. I figure it will be a couple of hours work. What's your typical fee?"

"Nothing. I wouldn't feel right charging you for this. You're donating your time, and I'm happy to do the same."

"That's not necessary. You're doing a job. I'm happy to pay."

"No," Sabrina said. "I insist. Just tell me what time to meet you, and I will gladly come with my camera and take the pictures you need. Now, if you want to order special prints, we can talk about the cost then. But you said it's for your website, so I suspect you'll be fine with digital prints. In which case, I wouldn't charge you for that."

"If you're sure," Mason said.

"Absolutely. I love that you're doing something so incredible." Maybe she didn't have him figured out as far as his personal life was concerned.

Maybe Nya was right. Her failed relationships, and the fact that her father hadn't been in her life in a meaningful way, had skewed her view of men.

"You have the address for the burn center?" Mason asked.

"Yes, I know where it is."

"How about you meet me at the front entrance at one?"

"I'll be there."

On Sunday at one p.m., Sabrina met Mason at the Ocean City Burn Center. Armed with her camera bag, she was ready to take as many pictures as necessary.

But she wasn't ready for the reality of what she would find in the children's ward.

Suddenly, all of the problems in her world seemed insignificant. The issues she had with her half siblings and her father were nowhere near as crushing as children having to go through multiple skin grafts.

Mason was greeted with warm smiles and excitement not only from the staff, but the patients. Sabrina saw toddlers with bandages over much of their bodies—who clearly had gone through unspeakable pain—light up when Mason gave them a stuffed animal.

Mason wore his official dress firefighter uniform, and in addition to handing a stuffed animal for each child, he also gave out coloring books on fire safety. He made the rounds, and Sabrina took photo after photo of him with not only the children, but also with the parents and the hospital staff.

Some of the children were too injured to get out of their beds, but Mason knelt down to be photographed by their sides. Other children whose injuries weren't as extensive were elated to sit on Mason's knee or stand beside him for their picture.

And with each shot she took, Sabrina's feelings about Mason changed. Some people did good deeds for the acclaim that came with it, but Sabrina could see that Mason was completely genuine. She was touched way down in her soul.

"Sabrina, come and meet Jenny."

Sabrina, who had pretty much stayed in the background acting solely as the photographer, lowered her camera and walked toward where Mason was sitting on the edge of a young girl's bed. Jenny had gauze around her entire right arm, and also on the right side of her head and face. She looked about four, and despite her obvious injuries, she wore the brightest smile.

"Hi." Jenny's little voice was filled with happiness. "I'm Jenny."

"Hi, Jenny." Sabrina went to her bedside. "I'm Sabrina."

"You're very pretty," Jenny told her.

"Not as pretty as you." The words seemed to tickle Jenny, and she giggled. "How do you like the bear?"

She squeezed it with her left arm. "I love it. I named her Princess. Because she looks like a princess."

"Indeed she does," Sabrina concurred. The bear wore a pink tutu and crown.

"Thank you so much for coming here today," the woman, clearly Jenny's mother, said. "It's made her day."

Sabrina wandered over to where she was sitting in a chair near the window and asked gently, "What happened?"

The woman's eyes filled with pain. "An electrical outlet caused a fire in her bedroom. We couldn't get to her in time. She endured third-degree burns to thirty percent of her body." Her eyes filled with tears as she spoke, but she forced a smile as she looked at her daughter. "She's already had two surgeries. There will be more. But already, she's improved so much. It hurts more than you can imagine seeing your child in pain and not being able to do anything about it. I keep thinking that I should have done something differently. Why didn't I get to Jenny faster that night?"

"No," Sabrina said to the woman. "Don't beat yourself up with thoughts like that. What happened was a tragedy you didn't anticipate."

"I know." The woman wiped at tears. "I just hate to see Jenny like this."

"I can only imagine. But she's here, and look at that smile."

The woman gazed fondly at Jenny, who was speaking with Mason. "I tell you, this center has been a godsend. The staff here has made all of the difference."

"I'm truly sorry for what your daughter is going through," Sabrina said. "What your family is going through. But I'm glad that you're getting the help you need here. And Jenny seems like a real fighter."

As if to accentuate her point, Jenny giggled. Sabrina glanced over her shoulder to see Mason prancing the bear around in front of her, playing some sort of game.

"Yes," her mother concurred. "She is."

Sabrina turned her focus toward Mason and Jenny and began taking photos of them as they interacted happily. The pictures captured hope and promise.

"Oh, wow," Sabrina said, looking at the LCD screen. "That's lovely."

"Can I see?" Jenny asked.

Sabrina approached her with the camera and showed her the photo of her and Mason, almost nose to nose as they shared a laugh. "Look at how beautiful you are, Jenny. You look like a princess yourself."

Jenny beamed as she looked at the picture, thrilled with the compliment. Then, looking up at Sabrina, she suddenly asked, "Is Mason your boyfriend?"

Sabrina's eyes whipped to Mason. "No." He met her gaze. "I just came with him to take some pictures today."

"I would be his girlfriend, but he said I'm too young," Jenny proclaimed.

"Is that so?" Sabrina asked.

"Uh-huh. And he said I have to wait until I'm at least twenty before I can marry him."

Jenny's comment caused them all to laugh in unison.

"Wow, you've got it all figured out, don't you?" Sabrina said with a smile.

"I like Captain Foley. He's nice. He always comes to visit me."

"I'd love to come back and visit you, too," Sabrina said. "You're such a brave little girl."

"You'll have to come back soon. My mom says I'll be going home soon."

"In about two weeks," her mother clarified.

"I bet you can't wait to go home," Sabrina said.

Jenny nodded. "I miss my dog. And my cat."

"I'll be sure to come back and visit you before you go home," Mason said to Jenny. "I'm gonna miss you here, but I'm really excited that you're getting better."

Sabrina smiled at her, but she felt emotion welling in her chest. How awful it was to be so young and dealing with such a horrific life-changing situation. She only hoped that with the loving support of her family, friends and medical staff, Jenny—and others like her—wouldn't allow physical scars to hold them back.

"Bye, Captain Foley," Jenny said in her sweet little voice. "Bye, Sabrina."

Mason and Sabrina said their goodbyes, and then exited the room. Sabrina went with Mason as he spoke to staff, updating them on his charitable efforts. While he did, Sabrina had to fight to keep it together. This hospital visit—and especially her time spent with Jenny—was overwhelming.

Once they left the building, Sabrina finally let out the emotion she had been holding in. Tears filled her eyes and she wiped them away. "Oh, my goodness," she said as she faced Mason. "That is just so heartbreaking. Those young kids. Babies."

"Yeah. Tell me about it. It's definitely hard to see them like that, but nonetheless, they always inspire me. With the pain they've endured, and the challenges they face daily, they still have an eternal optimism. As adults, we could learn a lot from them."

"You are so right," Sabrina agreed.

She was very impressed with all she'd experienced in

the past two hours. Not only with the children she'd seen, but also with Mason.

"What are you doing now?" Mason asked her.

"Besides going home and making a donation to your charity?" And crying.

"You must be hungry. Let me buy you dinner."

Sabrina didn't expect the question, at least not then.

"What can I say?" Mason went on when she didn't speak. "I'm interested in a bit more than just your photography skills. But you already know that."

"You're still interested," Sabrina said, noting that her voice sounded a little awe-filled.

"I know I came off strong before, so I'm trying a gentler approach." He smiled. "I don't know about you, but I haven't been able to put you out of my mind since the last time I saw you. If you're willing to go get a bite to eat—no fancy dinner, just something casual—I promise to be on my best behavior." When Sabrina didn't respond, he continued. "We'll hang out for a bit. Talk. Get better acquainted."

It seemed almost ridiculous to tell him no at this point. She definitely liked what she saw, even if her heart was afraid to open up to anyone.

Maybe she could follow this flirtation between them, see where it led and not worry about tomorrow. Have zero expectations and enjoy a bit of fun.

Because she was a woman with needs, needs that have been ignored for two years. She wasn't ready for a relationship, not with the realities of her business. She was busier than ever and she was happy with the progress of her studio, and she wanted nothing to slow her down. But could she make a little time for something extra? Certainly with a man like Mason, she didn't have to fear that he was going to want a commitment. He seemed like a nice guy, but she was certain that he had women coming out of the woodworks after him.

And that would suit her just fine. If she decided to pursue something physical with him.

Because it would only be physical. She couldn't allow herself to even think otherwise. Given Mason's good looks and easy charm, Sabrina knew that he was the kind of guy she would have to worry about forever. Was he cheating? Were women shamelessly throwing themselves at him when she wasn't around? Would he ultimately become bored with her?

But a no-strings-attached relationship…she supposed she could handle that.

"No answer?" Mason prompted.

"I suppose I can do dinner. That won't kill me."

Mason chortled. "Well, that's good to know. Because that would be a first. Dinner with me causing a woman to drop dead."

"As long as the dinner is just dinner…with no expectations."

"I expect to have some good conversation, and a nice meal. That okay?"

Sabrina quit while she was ahead. Every time she tried to set out ground rules, Mason twisted her words on her. Besides, she wanted to allow herself to just roll with the situation. See what might possibly happen. "What do you feel like eating?"

"Do you like sushi?"

Sabrina waved a dismissive hand. "Yes, but I'm not in the mood for that. I would just rather go somewhere casual. Maybe Los Panchos, if you like Mexican. Or something else quick and easy."

"Whatever the lady desires."

Chapter 9

They settled on Mexican as Sabrina had suggested, heading to the Los Panchos, which was nearby the burn center. As they entered the establishment, Sabrina's reservations regarding Mason were confirmed.

Female heads from within the restaurant turned almost instantly, as though women could sense that a fine specimen had entered the building. Eyes widened. Lips parted. Female friends began whispering with each other as they looked in Mason's direction.

Of course, with Mason wearing his dress firefighter's uniform, he was naturally getting attention from that. But the spark Sabrina saw in many of the female's eyes was purely sensual.

To Mason's credit, as they were led to a booth, he greeted people who stared with brief, courteous nods, and didn't hold the gazes of the women who brazenly checked him out.

Before they sat down, he removed his jacket and hung it on a hook outside their booth. Though Sabrina had already seen him with less clothing, she caught herself checking out his muscular form as his back was turned to her.

She quickly deflected her gaze once he turned back around. And as he sat in the booth opposite her, she pretended to be absorbed in the menu.

"What do you think you're going to have?" Sabrina asked.

"Probably chicken enchiladas. That's what I typically get when I come here."

"And I will probably have the fajitas. Which I get about ninety percent of the time," Sabrina added with a sheepish grin.

"Actually, maybe we can order the larger size and share? Beef and chicken?"

"I'm fine with that," Sabrina told him.

When their waitress came to the table, they placed the order for fajitas and a couple of sodas.

"So tell me," Sabrina said, taking a tortilla chip from the basket the waitress had brought to the table. "How did you end up starting your charity? I have to say, I'm really impressed."

"Like I said before, working in the field of firefighting, I see how people's lives are affected firsthand when a fire tragedy strikes. And during my volunteering, I—and other firefighters—realized that not a lot of donation money goes to fire victims. I'm trying to bring awareness to this issue, which is a lifelong one. Some of the people we saw are horribly burned. Burns to forty, fifty percent of their bodies. They will live with visible scars and sometimes even defects for the rest of their lives. I think it's an important issue."

Sabrina dipped the chip into salsa and then plopped it into her mouth. As she chewed, she stared at Mason with a sense of admiration. When she'd met him, he had been goofy. But there was a very serious side to him.

His sense of civic duty and responsibility went above and beyond what was necessary.

"It is an important issue, and I'm glad you asked me to come today," Sabrina said. "Make sure to give me your email address and I'll send you the photos tonight."

"Maybe I could even come by the studio and check them out on your computer."

The waitress arrived with their drinks, and Sabrina was glad for the distraction. She didn't know if Mason was thinking about coming to her studio today, but suddenly she remembered her dream where he tried to seduce her and became a bit anxious.

Mason lifted his glass. "Cheers," he said, and in reply, Sabrina raised her own glass. "To second chances to make a first impression."

"I'll drink to that." Sabrina clinked her glass against Mason's, and then sipped her cola.

Mason lowered his glass. "See—I told you I could be on better behavior."

"And you have been." Sabrina offered him a small smile. "You've shared your passion regarding your charity, but what you haven't told me is why you named the charity after your mother."

Mason's jaw tightened and undeniable pain flashed in his eyes. A few beats passed, and he said nothing, instead his gaze focused on a spot on the wood table.

"I'm sorry," Sabrina said. "If you don't want to tell me…"

"No, it's okay." Mason paused. "My mother died. Twenty years ago, when I was fifteen. She died in a house fire."

"Oh, Mason."

"My little brother, too," Mason went on. "He was five. There wasn't a working smoke alarm. They died of smoke inhalation."

Sabrina's heart broke for him. What a horrible tragedy. Instinctively, she reached for his hand, covered it with her own. "I'm so sorry."

Mason nodded, not meeting her gaze. "Thanks."

A beat passed, and Sabrina pulled her hand back, suddenly feeling awkward. "I can't even imagine…losing two family members at one time…it's so senseless."

"That it is," Mason agreed.

"You loved your mother a lot, didn't you? To name your charity in her honor…"

"She was a very special woman."

Sabrina didn't know what else to say. It was clear that the death of his mother and brother still affected him, despite the years. But how could a person make peace with something so tragic?

The waitress arrived with their order of fajitas, and her appearance broke the intensity of the somber moment.

"This smells delicious," Mason said. "I'm glad I went with the fajitas."

"My favorite dish here," Sabrina said.

Mason opened the container holding the tortillas, and put one on his plate. He then loaded on the grilled beef, grilled vegetables, salsa, cheese and guacamole.

Sabrina followed suit, opting for the chicken instead of beef. "This is *so* good. I haven't had fajitas in a long time," she announced after taking a bite.

"Amazing," Mason concurred.

They ate in silence for a few minutes, savoring the delicious fajitas.

"You've learned a lot about me today. I want to get to know more about you," Mason said as he began constructing a second fajita.

"Okay."

"So you're single? No boyfriend or even a guy you see occasionally?"

"Nope. I am most definitely single."

"I find that very hard to believe."

"It happens," Sabrina said, smiling sweetly. "What about you? Are you dating, married?"

"If I were, I wouldn't have asked you out."

"See—people are single. At this point in my life, I'm concentrating on my career."

"So for you it's always work, no pleasure?"

"It's not like I've *never* been involved with anyone. I was married, in fact."

"Wow." Mason's eyes bulged. He clearly wasn't expecting that response from her.

"Yeah. I was married for five years. It ended two years ago."

"Is he what stands between you and me getting to know each other better?"

Sabrina scoffed. "Definitely not. In fact, our divorce was the best thing that ever happened to me. Which is a really sad thing to say, I know. And I wish I didn't believe that. But we weren't good together." She paused. "Of course, when we split it was hard, but when I look back on our relationship I can see that he wasn't right for me. What I wanted, he couldn't give me. I kept hoping he would change. Then it dawned on me that I had settled... and I was miserable. That said, I would've fought to make the marriage work if he had wanted to. I loved him. I believe marriage should be forever. But when you're married to someone who doesn't believe the same thing, what can you do?"

She paused, remembering how her hopes and dreams had fallen apart with Lester. When she looked up, she saw that Mason was staring at her inquisitively.

"So, he was the one to leave?" he asked.

"Yes. And the truth is that when he dumped me, it was the best gift he could have given me. Of course, it didn't feel like that at the time. But he didn't believe in my dreams. He didn't support my career. Now, I'm no expert, but I don't think love is about sacrificing everything that's important to you to make the other person happy."

"No. I definitely don't think so. And I have to say, the loss is definitely his."

Mason held her gaze for a long while, and Sabrina

began to feel nervous. "I read an article about you," Sabrina said, wanting to take the focus off of her. "I didn't know that you used to be a basketball player."

"There's no reason you would."

"Not really. It sounds like you were a big deal in Ocean City. But, I didn't really pay attention to sports news. And I wasn't a basketball fan."

"It's not a requirement."

Sabrina took another bite of her fajita. When she was finished chewing, she said, "I guess it makes sense that you would play basketball. With your height, and your build. I'm not surprised." She paused. "But I am surprised that you left the NBA. I can't imagine many people who get drafted and do as well as you would leave at the end of a contract when teams across the nation were fighting to sign you." Her tone indicated it was a question, even though she'd made a statement.

"I just had enough. You're a photographer. I assume that's your passion, your calling. In a lot of ways, everyone expected me to play pro ball. I had the height, I was good. I followed what everyone else thought I should do. Was it exciting? Sure." He paused, and glanced away briefly. "But the tragedy that took my mother and brother never left me. There was always this burning desire in my heart to do something else, make a difference. As a little boy, I had always been excited when I saw that big red fire truck whiz by. I thought it would be great to grow up and become a firefighter. So, that childhood dream, combined with what happened to my mother and brother…well, I walked away from the NBA and I haven't looked back since."

Sabrina took another sip of her cola before speaking again. "Is that something you'd like me to highlight about you in the calendar?" For each firefighter, there was going to be a small bio about them. "That fact that you once played in the NBA, I mean."

"Not really. I'm a firefighter. That's it." Mason shrugged.

Sabrina looked at Mason as she ate another fajita. He was an enigma. He seemed extremely down-to-earth, which she liked.

"What?" Mason asked, sensing something else was on her mind.

"Do you ever regret leaving the NBA?" she asked.

"Not for a second," Mason answered immediately. "My life now has real purpose. And the good I do…being able to save lives…it's the best feeling in the world."

"You are a different kind of man," she found herself saying. "Once again, I'm very impressed." What he'd done was noble. And choosing to launch a charity showed that he had a heart of gold.

"So, what about you?" Mason asked. "How long have you been a photographer?"

"I've been playing with cameras since I was a little girl. It's just something I always loved to do. Take pictures. I dabbled with other things, mainly the idea of becoming a teacher, or perhaps going into law. I never wanted to be a teacher or a lawyer, but I considered those options because of—like you said—pressure from others. Mostly my mother. She wanted me to have a steady career. Being an artist is so unpredictable. There's no guarantee that you can make a living at it. But photography has always been what I was crazy about. From the time I got my first camera as a kid. So I pursued it. And I am happy to say the last couple of years my business has been better than ever." She grinned. "And here I am, now doing the firefighters' calendar. I'm happy."

"Your ex didn't support your work?"

"Initially, he did. Until—ironically—I started to become more successful. Then he complained about my hours, even talked about me quitting altogether so that I could be a stay-at-home mom." Sabrina shook her head, remembering his antics. "Given that he met me while I was taking pictures, I couldn't understand it."

"Have you dated since your divorce?" Mason asked.

"Here and there. Not as often as you date, I'm sure."

"Maybe I can't get dates."

Sabrina threw her head back and laughed. "Oh, that's likely. You're tall, gorgeous. Every woman in this city wants to date you."

"Yet you gave me a hard time when I asked you to dinner."

"That's because—" Sabrina stopped abruptly.

"Because?" Mason prompted. "And don't tell me it's about work. Because I think there's more to it than that."

"Well. Because." She hedged. She suddenly realized that if she told him what she really had thought, he would likely be offended.

"Because you looked at me and judged me?" Mason supplied. "Figured I'm a player? That I have a different woman for every day of the week?"

Sabrina said nothing, which said everything.

"Ahh, so that's it." Mason paused.

"It's not so much that I judged you," Sabrina began.

"But?"

"But guys like you typically don't have trouble finding a woman."

"Finding a woman is easy," Mason said. "Finding the right one is hard."

"You're really not seeing someone?" Sabrina asked, finding it hard to accept.

"I was kinda seeing someone a couple of months ago," Mason told her. "It wasn't serious. Like I said, if I were involved with someone, I wouldn't have asked you out."

"You wouldn't be the first man guilty of that," Sabrina said softly. And didn't she know it. The fact that she was conceived out of an adulterous relationship was something she would never be able to forget.

"You heard Jenny. She says I need a woman. So to make it clear, yes, I'm single. I don't have a wife I'm estranged from. I don't have a girlfriend who's wondering why I'm not calling her. The one woman I was seeing was out of town for a while, and has recently come back. She's called, but I haven't spoken to her yet. I'm not at all interested in picking up where we left off."

"You must have women throwing themselves at you wherever you go," Sabrina said.

"So that means I shouldn't be single? That I should just go for anyone?"

"No, of course not. But knowing women must find you attractive, I have to assume you're either superpicky, or very hard to get along with. Because the way I see it, there are always more women looking for a relationship than men. So any guy who's halfway decent should be able to find a good woman."

"Isn't that a little judgmental?"

"Is it? Guys have an easier time finding love."

"Not from where I'm sitting." He gave her a pointed look, and Sabrina felt a tingle in her abdomen. "Could I get involved with *any* woman? Sure. As a fireman, I meet a lot of women. As a basketball player, there wasn't a break from them. But the right kind of woman? One who isn't interested in how I can enhance her life with my check-book? Those kind of women are hard to find."

"Fair enough." She hadn't considered that he wouldn't enjoy the perks of being a hot commodity. "And you're right. I did judge you. The men I've known would take advantage of the fact that women threw themselves at them."

"You really think women throw themselves at me?"

Sabrina shrugged. "I mean, yeah."

"Then what's holding you back?" Mason's lips curled in a playful smile.

"Like I said, these days, I'm concentrating on my career."

Mason frowned. "That's no fun. But, hey, did you just admit that you *would* throw yourself at me, if not for work?"

Busted. "Mason…"

"So you want to be like a snail that never comes out of its shell? One that hides away forever?"

Sabrina didn't know what to say. She hadn't really thought of concentrating on her career as hiding. Could she throw herself at Mason? Most definitely. The man was fine, and a genuinely good guy. Which only made him more dangerous to her heart.

"It's not like I'm trying to hide."

Mason smiled. "Great. Then how about we do this again soon? But next time, let me take you to the kind of restaurant where we have to dress up."

Sabrina swallowed hard. He was asking her out on another date?

"I see the wheels turning in your brain," Mason said. "Trying to figure out a way to turn me down? Why don't you just say yes?"

"I…" Another date? A real one? She had guarded her heart for so long, she wasn't sure she knew how to let down the protective wall.

"You ready to leave?"

Sabrina narrowed her eyes at the unexpected question. "What?"

Mason flagged the waitress over. Even though she hadn't brought the bill over, he handed her more than enough money to cover the expense of the meal.

"Here," he said. "Take this. Keep the change."

The woman's eyes lit up. "You're sure?"

"Yes."

"Thank you," the woman said exuberantly. "Thank you so much!"

With the bill settled, Mason stood, lifted his jacket from the hook and then reached for Sabrina's hand. Sabrina stared at Mason in confusion as he led her outside.

"Why did you suddenly rush out of the restaurant?" Sabrina asked.

"I was anxious for dessert."

"What?" Sabrina narrowed her eyes, even more confused. "But we didn't even look at—"

Mason silenced her with a kiss. Sabrina's back went straight from the shock. As Mason's lips moved slowly and sensuously over hers, Sabrina gripped his biceps, allowing herself to enjoy the pleasure coursing through her body. As much as she wanted to protect her heart, she couldn't deny the serious attraction she had for him.

The gentle flicks of Mason's tongue over hers were making her delirious—it felt so good. And the way he was stroking both of her cheeks heightened the delicious sensations. She didn't want it to end.

All too soon, Mason eased back. His fingers continued to trail her jaw, his warm breath fanning her face. "That was the dessert I couldn't wait for. And I've never tasted anything sweeter."

Heat washed over Sabrina with the intensity of a wave from the Pacific Ocean. If she were a different person, she would grab Mason by the shirt and steal another kiss from him… The kind of kiss that would let him know where she wanted the night to lead.

But she didn't. Instead, she stared up at him, her breathing ragged.

Mason's lips curled in a slow smile. It was the kind of look that said he knew exactly what she wanted.

"I work tomorrow," he said. "But if you're interested in dinner on Tuesday or Wednesday, let me know."

Sabrina's eyes bulged. "Wh— Me?"

"Check your schedule. And if you've got the time, get back to me."

In other words, the ball was in her court.

If she wanted to see Mason again, she was going to have to let him know.

"I hope to hear from you soon."

With that, Mason turned and walked the short distance to his car, once again leaving Sabrina wanting a whole lot more than a searing kiss.

Chapter 10

"Let me get this straight," Nya said. She was in Sabrina's office, resting her bottom on the edge of the desk. "You went to the burn unit with him, and then suddenly you're out on a date?"

"It wasn't a date."

Nya gave her a look of doubt. "So you say. First, the man sent you a gazillion flowers. Then you go with him on this *job*." Nya made air quotes. "Which conveniently leads to you getting a bite to eat at a restaurant?"

"It was just two people getting some dinner after work. It's not like he set up the whole hospital visit just so he could take me to dinner. He was serious about hiring me. And I swear, after that trip to the burn center, if you ever hear me complain about anything again, slap me."

"That tough?"

"Worse than you can imagine. What those burn victims—especially the children—are going through. I'm so grateful Mason invited me."

"How was the dinner?" Nya asked.

"It was good. The fajitas were awesome."

"And the man? How was he?"

"Different than I expected," Sabrina admitted. "He's actually a very deep guy. There's a lot to like about him. He's very caring. I guess as a firefighter, fire victims are important to him. How many people not only volunteer their time to a cause, but actually begin their own charity to support it? He told me that he lost his mother and little brother to a house fire—"

"Oh, no!"

"It's awful, I know. I'm sure that loss inspired his charity. But however it came about, Mason is really incredible."

"You're right. That is incredible."

"He made a great point about the need for funding to burn units. So much funding and promotion goes into things like cancer research, heart and stroke disease. But burn victims' lives are irrevocably changed. And some of the kids I saw at the hospital were as small as months old. Honestly, it was crushing, and yet so inspiring. The work that staff does with the patients is phenomenal."

"Aww." Nya placed a hand over her heart. "That's wonderful. My goodness, when I was going out with Joe, he was as deep as a snail. All he cared about was if the teams he liked were winning, and of course, working out at the gym. I mean, it's fine to have fun things in your life, but Joe wouldn't know a social issue if it slapped him in the face."

Sabrina nodded, her mind on Mason. She had enjoyed their time at the burn unit, but what had happened afterward was just as impressionable on her.

Mainly, the kiss.

"What aren't you telling me?" Nya asked, her eyes filled with suspicion. "Because the look on your face…"

"We…well, we sort of kissed."

"Sort of kissed?" Nya all but shouted.

Sabrina shrugged. "Okay, so it was a real kiss. And it was great."

"Next time, lead with that! You go on about the visit to the burn center—which was great, yes—but next time, start with, 'I made out with Mason!'"

"It wasn't like we made out. It was a kiss. And it was… it was really nice."

"Yes!" Nya pumped a fist in the air.

"And I guess this is as good a time as any to tell you that it wasn't the first time."

Nya jumped off the desk. "What did you just say?"

Sabrina gave her friend a sheepish look. "I didn't tell you, I know."

"After how you went on about how he wasn't your type?"

"He was leaving the office after that meeting we had. And the next thing I knew, he was kissing me. He did the same thing after we left the restaurant."

"Girl, am I not supposed to be your best friend? And you don't tell me this?"

"After the first time, I didn't really know what to think. I figured it was just about…I don't know, him proving that he could? But yesterday, I saw a whole other side to him. So when he kissed me outside the restaurant…" Sabrina's voice trailed off as she remembered the feel of Mason's lips on hers.

"You're smitten. Look at you!"

"But nothing's changed," Sabrina said after a moment, coming down from cloud nine. "Would dating him be fun in the short-term? Absolutely. But I have to think long-term and be realistic. You should have seen when we walked into the restaurant. Women looked at him as if they'd never seen a man before. Can you imagine when he's on the job, rescuing people? Heck, what is life like for him when he's just walking down the street."

"You and that stupid rule about not dating a man who's too fine. For one thing, why are you even thinking about long-term? If I were you, I would be thinking about getting some immediate action. It's been way too long. I'd be worried that your parts are no longer working."

"Okay, that's enough." Sabrina turned her attention

back her computer screen. "I have some photos to go through before the Fords come in."

"Of course. Now you're getting rid of me."

"I have work to do," Sabrina said. "And so do you," she added, giving Nya a pointed look. "Lunch is over."

"All right. I know when I'm not wanted," Nya said playfully. She headed toward the door, and then stopped. "Hey, here's an idea. Why don't you ask him to go to your father's birthday party with you?"

Sabrina's stomach suddenly lurched. Her father's birthday party…something she wasn't looking forward to.

Out of the blue, her father had invited her to his sixty-fifth birthday bash. Sabrina had naturally been stunned by the invite and declined. She had kindly reminded her father that his family wouldn't want her there, anyway.

"You're my family, too," Gerald had told her. "And I'm turning sixty-five. That is a milestone birthday. God only knows how many years I'll have left. And I want you to be more a part of my life. You come. I'll deal with my family."

So, reluctantly Sabrina had agreed to attend the celebration. But she was still wary. And to bring Mason with her?

"You're not serious," she said to Nya.

"Sure I am. From what you've described, he sounds like an amazing man. And the perfect date for your father's birthday bash. Since I'm not going to be in town, I think Mason would be a great replacement."

Sabrina shook her head. "No. I'm not going to ask him—"

"I know you don't want to go to your father's birthday party alone. And now you have a solution. You've already broken the ice with Mason. You've had your first date. You've kissed him—twice—and I'll forgive you for not telling me about the first time as long as you make sure it doesn't happen again." Nya smiled sweetly. "Ask him. You shouldn't *not* go to your father's birthday party because I can't go with you. Go—with Mason."

Sabrina was conflicted. After receiving that letter from Julia, she had decided not to go to her father's sixty-fifth birthday celebration, despite his earlier appeal. Part of the reason she had reached out to her sister online was because she had hoped to gauge whether or not the family had still despised her before attending the event. If Julia had been receptive, then the party could have been the first step in forging a new relationship with her siblings.

But Julia had made it clear there would be no relationship.

"After Julia's letter to me, I wasn't planning to go at all," Sabrina said. "Whether or not you could come with me."

Nya planted her hands on her hips and started back toward her. "He's your father, too. It's not right, you having to feel like the unworthy daughter all these years. He asked you to go, and I think you should go. Obviously, you don't want to go alone, and you can't bring your mother. Your father only turns sixty-five once. Trust me, if mine were still around, I would go. Nothing would keep me away. If my daddy had lived to see sixty-five, I would be there to celebrate."

Sabrina made a face as pain squeezed her heart. Nya's words were getting to her. She knew her friend was right. Gerald Parker was her father, too, and she had a right to be at the party to celebrate this milestone birthday with him. After all, he wanted her there.

"Ask him," Nya insisted. "See if he's available. If he says no, then I can understand why you would decide not to bother going. But if he is available…why not go? Your father's side of the family has shut you out of his life for way too long."

The more Sabrina listened to Nya's reasoning, the more she was swayed. "You know what? I think I just might do that."

The fire alarm went off at the station, and Mason, Tyler and the rest of the firefighters on his shift jumped out of bed and sprang into action. Mason didn't like being jarred from sleep, but he was used to this particular aspect of the job. He quickly went to the pole and slid down to the firehouse's bay.

"Engine two, ladder two, battalion two," dispatch was saying over the loud speaker. "Respond to structure fire at three-zero-four King Street."

On the main level of the firehouse, Mason ran to his turnout gear and slipped his feet into the boots. Mason pulled up the pants, and then got into the heavy protective coat as efficiently as possible. He and his colleagues were in their respective trucks within a minute.

In the truck, dispatch confirmed the location of the structure fire, and knowing that stretch of King Street, Mason was certain they were en route to another restaurant.

The victims of the last restaurant fire had confirmed that a serial arsonist with a vendetta was at large. The husband and wife, transplants from New York, had taken their life's savings and put it into opening a steakhouse. Before the fire, they had also received two letters telling them to close up shop and head out of town.

When the engine pulled up to the scene of the fire three minutes after leaving the station, Mason saw complete chaos. Restaurant staff and patrons alike were out on the sidewalk, moving around in a state of confusion. Some were crying, some gasping for air, some were hugging each other in support. All of them looked toward the burning building; their faces said that they couldn't comprehend what had happened.

Tyler was busy getting the hoses off of the truck, as the other firefighters from the engine truck quickly pulled them loose. The firefighters from the ladder truck were grabbing axes and other tools to help ventilate the building.

"Is anybody inside?" Mason asked the crowd at large. Word from dispatch had been that everyone was out, but he always asked to make sure.

"Yes," a few people replied.

"I think so," said another.

Mason didn't like uncertainty. He had his thermal imaging camera in hand and was trying to determine the best place to enter the building when a woman frantically ran up to him.

"My manager's still in there! She went back in to make sure everyone got out, and she hasn't come back out yet!" the lady screamed.

"You're sure?"

"Yes, I'm sure." The woman sobbed. "She also said something about getting to the safe in the office."

An expletive popped into Mason's mind, but he kept it contained. When would people learn that material things could be replaced?

"Stephenson, we've got to go in. Someone's inside! Get the battering ram!" As Stephenson ran off, Mason spoke into his radio, "Chief Adeline, do *not* cut the power yet. We've got a victim inside and I need eyes in there." Mason then looked at the terrified woman and asked, "Where's the office?"

"On the far right side, at the back."

Mason took off, with Stephenson quickly following him. For safety reasons, no firefighter was to enter a building without a partner. The first blasts of water began to hit the building as Mason burst through the front door.

Angry orange flames ravaged the structure.

"Ocean City Fire Department, anybody inside?" Mason bellowed.

No response.

He had the thermal imaging camera on and was scanning the area around him, but prayed no one was in this part of the restaurant. One breath of this scorching heat was enough to fry a person's lungs and would mean certain death.

He moved quickly, heading for the back, right corner. The flames provided light and he found his way to a narrow corridor where the ceiling was burning, thick smoke made it hard to see. But because the electricity had not yet been cut, Mason was able to see the shaft of light coming from beneath a door on the right-hand side.

He hustled to the door, and once again yelled, "Ocean City Fire Department! If you can hear me, back away from the door!"

Then he turned the knob. A nanosecond later, he saw the woman in a hump on the floor. The door to the safe was open, and some cash was strewn on the floor. Though this room was closed and had been protected from the flames, it hadn't been protected from the fire. He ran to the woman while Graham Stephenson worked to open the exit door, which was thankfully beside the office. The chatter from the radio told him the roof of the restaurant had been ventilated, so the exit door could be opened without causing a backdraft.

"The door won't open!" Stephenson bellowed.

"Try again!" Mason ordered.

"It won't budge!" Stephenson said after a few more seconds.

There was no time. With the back exit off-limits, Mason had no choice but to carry the woman through the most dangerous part of the restaurant. Burning ceiling tiles had no doubt already fallen, a danger to the woman who was not dressed in the protective gear.

But he had no other choice.

"Okay," Mason began, "then we've got to go back the way we came in." Quickly, he took the respirator from his protective helmet and covered the woman's mouth. He couldn't allow her to breathe in the air and deadly gasses.

Then, holding his own breath, he ran through the flames and falling debris. It felt like minutes passed, but in no more than thirty seconds, he was bursting through the front doors with the woman in his arms. He ran almost to the street before he had to gasp in a desperate breath for air.

People began to cheer, but Mason was almost oblivious to it. The medics had the gurney out, and that was his only focus. He gently laid the woman onto it, and two medics instantly began to tend to her. He stared down at her as he breathed in more of the cool night air. He could see the burns to her blouse. He hadn't been able to protect her from the flames, but it was the breath of life he was so frantically waiting to see...

"We've got a pulse," Sarah Jeffries announced. Then she beamed at Mason. "She's alive."

Waves of relief washed over Mason. The cheers grew even louder.

"Good job, Captain," Ian McIntyre, the second paramedic said.

Stephenson slapped Mason's back. "Congrats."

Stephenson then started toward the other firefighters, who were holding hoses. And Mason began to follow behind him.

"Not so fast," Ian told him. "Let me check your vitals."

"I'm fine," Mason assured him.

"You had your respirator disconnected. I need to be sure."

"Help the victims. Bandage her burns. I've got a fire to put out."

And as he hurried toward the building with the rest of his team, a smile broke out on his face. People were still clapping and whistling, and some called out the word *hero*.

It was a nice feeling, definitely, but his greatest reward was knowing that he had saved the manager's life. And that was why he did this job. To make a difference. To save lives.

Unlike the lives he had not been able to save that day twenty years ago.

Chapter 11

Nya sauntered into Sabrina's office and plopped the paper down on her desk. "Check it out."

Sabrina's gaze went from her computer screen to the newspaper. She scanned the headline, her eyes widening as she did.

TRUE HERO:
Mason Foley, Fire Captain, saves life at third restaurant blaze in three weeks.

Sabrina then read the article, which touted Mason's bravery. Despite the danger to himself when the entire restaurant was ablaze, Mason had charged into the building in a valiant effort to save the life of the person trapped inside.

"Wow," Sabrina muttered, once she was finished reading the article.

"Can you believe that man ran into the restaurant and saved that woman?" Nya asked, shaking her head in amazement. "Like the article says, firefighters are true heroes. It's obvious that Mason isn't just a good-looking guy, he's a great person."

"He certainly is," Sabrina concurred. He had literally risked his own life in order to save the manager who had been trapped inside.

"Have you called him yet?" Nya asked. The way she

squinted her eyes as she looked at Sabrina said that she already knew the answer to her question.

"No."

"Why not?"

"You only suggested it yesterday."

"What are you waiting for? A lunar eclipse?"

"No. Of course not." Sabrina pushed her chair back and stood. "Truthfully?" Suddenly the idea felt awkward. *Hey, want to go to my father's birthday celebration with me?* "I don't know."

"You think he's going to say no?"

"Maybe."

Nya rolled her eyes. "Ridiculous. But if you were afraid to call to ask him out, now you can call and tell him how proud you are of him. Heroism like that certainly deserves a phone call, right? Then mention your father's party and ask if he wants to go with you."

"Okay, okay." Sabrina held up both hands. "I guess I was a little bit shy about doing it, but I will."

"Yay." Nya clapped her hands. "Right now?"

"Soon."

Nya made a face. "I will," Sabrina assured her. And she would. The truth was, she hadn't been able to put Mason out of her mind since their date. Her body had been burning up each night since their last kiss.

But Sabrina was at war with herself. Her mind kept reminding her that a man like Mason was not dating material, not in the least. But she was undeniably attracted to him from the way he made her feel.

After reading about his heroism, she was drawn to him even more. It was a truly attractive quality. Sabrina had labeled him simply a good-looking playboy, but she could see how unfair that had been. Surely getting to know him more would be a good thing.

"I'm going to be on your case," Nya said. "I'm going to make sure you don't chicken out. Call that man!"

Sabrina went back to her desk. "Okay, I will. Actually, I have a better idea."

"What's that?"

Sabrina picked up the phone. "You'll see."

Nya went around to Sabrina's side as she made the call. Two rings later, someone at the firehouse picked up.

"Um, hello," Sabrina said. "This is Sabrina Crawford, the photographer working on the firefighter's calendar. I'm just wondering when Mason Foley will be in again?"

"Actually, he's here right now."

Sabrina swallowed. "He is?"

"Yeah. He came in to work out at the gym. He'll probably be here for an hour."

"Thank you," Sabrina said to the man.

When she hung up, Nya looked at her expectantly. "Well?"

"He's there. I didn't think he would be."

"But you didn't talk to him."

"That's because I plan to go see him." Sabrina looked at the time on her computer screen. "I've got forty-five minutes before my next appointment." She was already rising from her chair. "Enough time to bring Mason a special treat."

Sabrina left her office and hurried over to Jean's Treats, where she bought a delectable brownie for Mason. As an added touch that she hoped didn't come off as corny, she asked Jean to write "Hero" across the top in white icing.

Then she got into her SUV and drove to the firehouse. It was within walking distance, but she didn't have the time.

Her heart picked up speed as she got out of her vehicle and started into the firehouse bay. A firefighter she hadn't seen before was washing one side of the ladder truck. She offered him a smile, and then kept going.

Once inside the bay, she noticed a firefighter named Dave, whom she had photographed for the calendar, standing beside the engine truck. Upon seeing her in his peripheral vision, he turned toward her.

"Dave, right?" Sabrina said, approaching him.

"That's right." Grinning, he lowered the clipboard in his hand. "Sabrina, how are you?"

"Good, good."

"How's the calendar coming?"

"Excellent," she told him. "I understand Mason Foley is in the gym. I brought something for him. Would you mind calling him for me?"

"No problem," Dave said. "Gimme a minute."

Dave headed through a door and out of her view, and Sabrina stood there waiting, shifting her weight from foot-to-foot. Good grief, why was she so nervous?

Maybe this is corny, she said to herself. *Mason's going to think this is stupid. Why didn't I just call him, or better yet, send a text?*

"Wow, look who it is."

At the sound of his voice, Sabrina's stomach fluttered. And then she turned. Seeing Mason, tall and gorgeous and wearing that charming smile, sent a jolt of heat straight to her nether region.

"H-hi," she stuttered, wondering how on earth anyone could look so incredible. He was wearing a pair of navy-blue athletic shorts and a sleeveless white muscle shirt. She had seen his chest and biceps during the photo shoot, but now she was getting a tantalizing view of his legs. Long and ripped with muscles, they looked powerful. Mason was one helluva man.

"What are you doing here?" he asked, walking up to

her. His gaze flitted between the small cake box in her hand and her face.

"I came to see you," she said, and extended the cake box. "This is for you. I figured a hero deserved a special treat."

"Thank you." Mason took the box from her and opened it. When he looked inside, a smile broke out on his face.

"I hope you don't think it's silly," she said.

"*Hero.* I love it."

A slow smile spread on Sabrina's face. "You do?"

"Yep. But I love even more that you're here. You had me thinking I wasn't going to hear from you again."

"I...well, I was just waiting for the right time. And after your heroic feat last night, I figured today was the perfect time."

"Can I take a bite?" Mason asked.

"It's for you."

Mason lifted out the brownie and took a huge bite, then sighed with pleasure. "This is delicious."

Sabrina glanced at Mason's muscular arms and thought the same.

"What are you doing now?" Mason asked. "I'm just finishing my workout. Let me take you to lunch."

"Actually, I can't stay," Sabrina said. "I have an appointment soon. I just wanted to come by and tell you that I'm proud of you." She paused. "Every day, I'm learning more and more about you and I'm more and more fascinated."

Mason's eyes held hers, and she could see the desire there. Desire that matched what she was feeling.

"You sure you don't have time for lunch?" he asked.

"I wish I did, but I have to get back."

Mason's gaze went from her eyes to her lips. "Maybe I can walk you back, then?"

"I drove. I was short on time."

"All right. Then let me walk you to your car."

Sabrina inhaled a shuddery breath as she started out of the bay, Mason walking beside her. It was clear, based on the look he'd given her, that he wanted to kiss her again.

And she wanted the same thing.

At her vehicle, Sabrina faced him. "Like I said, I'm proud of you. You did good last night."

"Thank you."

"Everyone loves a hero," she added with a sheepish smile.

"You know I want to kiss you right now."

Sabrina's eyes flew to Mason's.

"I know," he said. "I can't." He looked over his shoulder, and was rewarded with his fellow firefighters waving, grinning and flashing thumbs-up signs. "Not with the all of those bozos behind me." He softened the derogatory comment with a smile. "But that doesn't mean I don't want to. Damn."

"Well, maybe you'll get the chance if you're free on Saturday night," she found herself saying.

Mason gave her a puzzled look. "Saturday night? Are you inviting me to dinner?"

Had Sabrina really just said what she thought she'd said? "Actually," she began, not looking into Mason's eyes. "I was thinking that maybe we could do something other than dinner?"

"Oh?" Mason raised an eyebrow.

Suddenly, Sabrina realized how she was coming across. She must have sounded as though she was ready to skip past dinner or dating and head straight to bed.

"There's an event I'd like to attend, but I don't want to go alone." She paused, feeling a little awkward. "I know this is going to sound crazy, and if it does, feel free to say no and I'd still be happy to take you up on your dinner invitation. But there's an event I was putting off going to, and maybe you could go with me?"

Sabrina realized that one of her eyes was closed, and the other was squinting at him—and it had nothing to do with the sun. Good grief, why had she listened to Nya's suggestion.

"So, you want me to be your date to an event." Mason raised an eyebrow. "What is it, a wedding?"

"It's a birthday celebration, actually. There'll be dinner, dancing. We wouldn't even have to stay long. I just want to show my face."

"This sounds mysterious," Mason said, eyeing her with suspicion. "Will there be some ex-boyfriend there that you hope to make jealous? Because I'm not down with that."

"God, no. It's my father's sixty-fifth birthday celebration. And it's sort of a long story, one I can't get into right now. But let's just say the situation is awkward, and I wasn't necessarily going to go. But now I'm considering it. Only if I have a date." She shrugged. "So, what do you say?"

"You're in luck," Mason told her. "I'm off Saturday."

"You are?" Sabrina asked, knowing that she sounded more excited than she'd intended.

"Uh-huh. And I'd be happy to go with you."

"Oh, good." Sabrina was relieved. Knowing that Mason would be there for her was a huge weight off her shoulders.

"Just tell me the time and where to pick you up."

Pick her up? She hadn't figured that he would pick her up. She hadn't thought beyond the scenario of asking him to go with her. But of course, he wouldn't meet her there.

"Right," Sabrina said. "How about I call or text you later with the details."

Sabrina turned and opened her car door. "I guess it's safe to say that you like me. At least a little."

Sabrina got behind the wheel of her truck. "I'm not asking you to go as a boyfriend or anything, just my date."

Mason's reply was a wide grin. "Oh, I think you like me, too."

"I'll call you later," was all Sabrina said before closing the door and slipping her sunglasses on.

As she began to back out of the parking spot, she had to acknowledge that she was sending Mason mixed messages. One minute she was all but offering him the opportunity to kiss her again at her father's party. The next she was telling him that she was only inviting him as a friend.

She had no clue why she was trying to downplay her attraction to him, when the reality was she would love the opportunity to kiss him again.

No, that was a lie. She knew why.

As attracted as she was to him, she was afraid of her feelings. They had come hard and fast, and she couldn't entirely trust them. She knew that the risk of getting hurt was superhigh.

A part of her wanted to keep him at bay. But another part of her wanted him to rip her clothes off and make wild love to her.

That was the part that scared her.

Chapter 12

Sabrina was a bundle of nerves as she got ready for her father's sixty-fifth birthday celebration. Mason was due to arrive in minutes. She was wearing an above-the-knee black dress with a lace overlay. A silver choker encrusted with clear crystals adorned her neck. She wore subtle silver hoop earrings. On her wrist, she had several silver bangles, some with crystals, some glittery. She had loosely curled her hair so that there were drop curls framing her face, and she swept the back up into a bun.

Normally, Sabrina wasn't one to go all out with her makeup. But tonight, she wanted to wow, so she did her best to accent her eyes, which she had always been told were her best feature. After watching an instructional video online, Sabrina had gone to the mall and picked up liquid liner, a myriad of eye shadows and two different mascaras that promised to lengthen and thicken.

Now, with her attempt at a dramatic evening look complete, Sabrina stared at her reflection and smiled. The results of her efforts were eyes that popped in a seriously sexy way, and gorgeous lengthy lashes.

She hardly recognized herself.

She applied a dark lipstick she had picked up at the mall and topped it off with gloss. She stood back and checked out her entire appearance.

She looked stunning.

The doorbell rang, and Sabrina's stomach lurched. *Mason.*

She fiddled with the strands of her hair for a brief moment, making sure they were in place. Then she headed out of the bathroom and picked up the sparkly silver clutch she'd placed on her kitchen table, along with the gold gift bag that held the present for her father. She was already wearing her shoes, silver strappy sandals that matched her accessories. All set, she made her way down the stairs and opened the door at the side of the building.

Her first glimpse of Mason caused her heart to falter. He was in a black blazer, black dress pants and a pale pink dress shirt. Freshly shaven, he looked as if he had stepped off a runway in Milan and simply showed up at her door.

He was absolutely scrumptious.

But it was the way his eyes roamed over her from head to toe that made her feel a tingle throughout her body.

His eyes settled on hers again. "Wow, you look *amazing.*"

Sabrina's drew in a deep breath. It had been so long since she had gotten dressed up to go on a date, and Mason's compliment made her feel incredible.

"Seriously," he went on. "You're absolutely gorgeous."

Sabrina felt a rush of excitement. Not just because Mason was flattering her, but also because she was thrilled to spend more time with him. Her first date with Mason had been casual and spur of the moment, but tonight was a big to-do. It seemed as though they had taken a huge step forward.

"You look pretty dapper yourself," Sabrina told him. "Very hot." She then looked downward and chuckled softly, slightly embarrassed. "I mean, very handsome."

"If you think I look hot, don't be ashamed to say so." His light-hearted grin put her at ease. "I say we make an attractive couple."

He extended his hand to her, and she took it. Then he guided her out of her door. She took a moment to lock it, and once she was finished, he slipped his arm around her waist as he led her to his Mercedes.

"Thank you again for doing this, by the way," Sabrina said once they got to his car. "I really appreciate you being able to accompany me to this party."

"Thank you for inviting me." Mason opened the passenger door for Sabrina, guided her inside and then closed it. Moments later, he was getting into the car on the opposite side. As he started to drive, smooth jazz filled the airwaves. "This is a CD, but if you want me to put on the radio, let me know."

"Ella Fitzgerald? Don't you dare change the CD."

"You like the First Lady of Song?"

Sabrina cut her eyes as she looked at Mason. "Is that a rhetorical question?"

He grinned. "All right, then."

The rifts of the previous song ended, and the familiar notes of a trumpet began to sound. "Oooh," Sabrina said. "'Summertime' with Ella Fitzgerald and Louis Armstrong. I love this."

"You know your jazz."

"Sometimes I think I was born in the wrong era," Sabrina said. "Billie Holiday, Sarah Vaughan, Nat King Cole… Need I go on?"

"I knew there was a reason I liked you," Mason said.

Sabrina was actually surprised that he wasn't blaring hip-hop, but didn't say so. Everything she had once thought about him had already proven to be untrue.

"You have any hip-hop CDs?" she asked instead.

"Sure. I love old school, but it's not my choice for everyday listening. I prefer jazz any day."

Sabrina eased her head back against the headrest and listened to the sultry sounds of Ella and Louis, impressed with Mason's choice of music. Only once the song was over did she speak again. "Are you ever affected by people's opinions of your choice to give up your career in the NBA?"

"Not for a minute," Mason answered without preamble. "I know many people don't understand, and that includes much of my family. But for me, being a firefighter gives me a sense of purpose."

Sabrina sensed there was more to his desire to become a firefighter and not for the first time. Perhaps the loss of his mother and brother had driven him into this career. She picked up on a trace of sadness in him, but wasn't quite sure if she was just misreading him. Years had passed since the tragic fire that had claimed his beloved family members, but did he still have a hole in his heart because of the loss?

It wasn't something she wanted to ask him, not right now, anyway. She had enough on her plate given where they were headed.

As they neared the venue, Sabrina's anxiety level rose. Mason pulled up in front of the restaurant, Le Ciel, stopping at the valet stand. A man wearing white gloves, black dress pants and a black vest over a white dress shirt immediately came to the passenger's side of the car. He opened the door and offered Sabrina a hand to help her out of the vehicle. Then he went around to the driver's side and opened the door for Mason. As Mason exited, the valet offered him a ticket for his car, which Mason stuck in the inner pocket of his crisp blazer. He then handed over his keys and went to join her on the sidewalk.

Sabrina didn't realize that she was standing paralyzed until Mason said, "Hey. Are you all right?"

"I—I—don't know."

Mason moved in front of her and placed his hands on her shoulders. "Why do you look like you're scared to

death? You did say something about there being a story
that you didn't want to get into, and now I'm wondering
if we should be here."

"No, it's okay." Sabrina steeled her shoulders. "It's okay.
I'm just…nervous."

"You want to tell me why?" Mason looked completely
concerned. "Is there someone here you don't want to see?"

Sabrina released a ragged breath. "There are things I
haven't told you about my father. Namely that he has another family. They don't like me. Now still isn't a good
time to get into it, but my father wanted me here. Even
though I'm sure they don't. But since he's my father, too,
and he's only going to be sixty-five once, I'm here."

"This is a party," Mason said. "I'm sure everyone will
be able to put aside their differences for the sake of your
father."

Sabrina inhaled deeply. "Yes, I'm sure." She forced a
smile. "Everything will be fine. And I don't plan to stay
all evening. I just want to see my father, give him this gift.
Hang out for a bit. Then we can leave early. Maybe get a
drink somewhere else."

Mason rubbed her shoulders. He looked relieved. "Okay,
that sounds like a good plan. Play it by ear. If things get
uncomfortable—and I'm sure they won't—then we can
leave. Ready to go inside?"

Sabrina nodded. Then she slipped her arm through Mason's and held it. It felt good to cling to him as she went
through the doors of the restaurant.

The restaurant was beautiful. It had a brick facade on
the inside, and the decor was gorgeous. There was an ele-
ment of classic elegance and sophistication, as well as mod-
ern chic. The lighting fixtures, with their unique shapes
and countless glass beads, were like pieces of art. Each
table was adorned with a white satin top, on top of which
were candles in red glass containers.

The entire restaurant had been rented out for her father's birthday bash. No surprise. Being a city councilor, he had clout.

"It looks lovely." Sabrina glanced around. People were laughing and smiling. Some were gathered in small groups as they chatted, while others strolled through the crowd, mingling. Waitstaff wandered through the room with trays of hors d'oeuvres and platters of champagne flutes. This party was definitely a classy affair.

A smiling female waitress approached Sabrina and Mason, offering them champagne. Both Sabrina and Mason accepted a glass.

"Which one is your father?" Mason asked.

"Ah, there he is." Sabrina pointed to the front of the restaurant, close to where a jazz quartet was playing. "They really went all out," she muttered.

Her father caught her eye, and he beamed. He started toward her, and Sabrina walked toward him. Balloons announcing happy sixty-fifth birthday were interspersed throughout the corners of the room, creating a truly festive atmosphere.

"Sabrina." Her father spread his arms wide as she walked into his embrace. "I'm so glad you came."

"Hi, Daddy."

He held her in a long hug, as though he didn't want to let her go. They didn't see each other that often, and Sabrina wished they were closer. But it was always good to see him, whenever they could make the time.

Pulling apart from him, she extended the gift bag. "This is for you."

"You didn't have to bring me anything."

"I wanted to." She squeezed his hand. "Happy birthday."

Her father looked up at Mason. "Who's this?"

"Daddy, this is my friend, Mason. Mason, this is my father, Gerald."

"Mason Foley, right?" her father asked. "Drafted to San Antonio, but walked away from the NBA after your contract ended."

"Yes, sir." Mason extended his hand. "It's a pleasure to meet you, Mr. Parker"

Gerald looked intrigued. "How do you know my daughter?"

"We met at the firehouse—"

"I've been contracted to do the annual firefighter's calendar—"

Sabrina and Mason looked at each other and smiled, both of them having spoken at the same time. Sabrina said, "Go ahead. You tell him."

"Your daughter has taken photos of me for the annual firehouse calendar. I'm a Fire Captain at Station Two."

Gerald nodded. "That's right. I heard that you had become a firefighter. And if memory strikes me, didn't I read an article about you being a hero recently?"

"You certainly keep up on current events," Mason said with an easy smile.

"I try my best."

"Clearly," Sabrina began, "Mason doesn't want to brag on himself. That's one of the things I've really come to enjoy about him," she added, meeting his gaze. She offered him a smile before she faced her father again. "He's a true hero, Daddy. And he's even started a charity to benefit the Ocean City Burn Center."

Gerald's eyes lit up. "Impressive."

Mason almost seemed embarrassed by the attention. "You're daughter's the one who's impressive. Her photography... I'm blown away by it."

"Thank you," Sabrina said, feeling a rush of pride.

"I love my daughter's work, as well," Gerald said to Mason.

As her father and Mason spoke, Sabrina gazed around

the restaurant. That's when she saw her sister and brother standing with their mother near the far right side at the front of the room. Marilyn was glaring at her.

Sabrina quickly looked back at her father. "Daddy, shall we sit anywhere?"

"I saved a spot for you at the table next to mine," he explained.

Sabrina shook her head. "No. I'm not sure that's the best idea."

Before she could explain why, her father looked over his shoulder. He had to have picked up on the look of displeasure on his wife's face.

"Sabrina, you're my daughter," he said when he faced her again. "If I want you close to me—"

"I don't want to upset anyone. Mason and I can sit somewhere in the back. It's fine." She forced a smile. "I'm here, and that's what matters."

"Marilyn will be fine, too," Gerald stressed.

Now was not the time to tell her father about the letter. "I would feel better if Mason and I sat at a different table. Is that okay?"

Her father seemed unhappy, but nodded with resignation. "You're right, you're here, and that's what matters."

When her father walked away from her, Mason asked, "What was that about?"

Sabrina turned. "Why don't we sit over there." She pointed to a table near the wall, closer to the back of the restaurant near the windows. And before Mason could even respond, she began walking in that direction.

"You don't want to say hi to your father's family?" Mason asked. "It may seem impolite if you don't. And be a cause of further contention, which it seems you want to avoid."

Sabrina scoffed. "Trust me, you have no idea. Going

over there to say hi is likely to get me slapped. They want nothing to do with me."

Mason looked in the direction of the front, then back at Sabrina. "I guess you'll tell me later?"

"Yes, later."

They sat at the table Sabrina had selected, and Mason took her hand in his. She knew he was offering her comfort, and she appreciated it. Her heart was racing. Her level of anxiety was off the chain. She glanced toward her half siblings, and saw that they weren't even looking at her. She imagined that as far as they were concerned, she didn't exist.

Sabrina was glad when the waitstaff came around and took orders, and things got underway. As the appetizers were being served, friends and colleagues went up to the microphone and spoke wonderful things about Gerald Parker. A dedicated family man. Dedicated to his community. Having been a city councilor for a long time, he was well respected in Ocean City.

But for so long, Sabrina had been his dirty little secret. He hadn't openly accepted her. Even though he did now, Sabrina couldn't be sure the average person even knew of her connection to him. Except, of course, for the family that despised her.

Sabrina focused on Mason, especially as they each ate a plate of Forchu Lobster, which was absolutely delectable. As the waitstaff collected dinner plates and took dessert orders, the floor opened up for speeches. Julia and Patrick went up together, speaking of their father with the highest regard. Which caused a familiar lump to lodge in Sabrina's throat. She had never been raised with that father, and wished that she knew him as well as her half siblings did.

When Julia and Patrick returned to their seats, Mason looked at her. "Are you going to go up?"

Sabrina's level of unease rose. She had been wonder-

ing the entire evening if she would get up and say something in tribute to her father. She wanted to, but she didn't
know if she should.

Upon seeing that no one else was immediately going
up to the microphone, Sabrina finally began to push her
chair back. Swallowing, she rose. It was her father's birthday, and she was there, she should at least say a few words.

As she made her way to the front of the restaurant to
speak, she saw her father's wife quickly rise from her table
and start toward her with determination in her steps. Before Sabrina could reach the microphone, Marilyn took
her by the upper arm and whisked her down the hallway
toward the restroom. Her fingers gripped around her arm
like a vice, Marilyn pushed the bathroom door open and
dragged Sabrina inside.

Marilyn leveled an intense look of disgust on Sabrina.
"How *dare* you?"

Sabrina stared at her in horror. "How dare I? You just
grabbed me and ushered me away in front of everyone?
And let go of my arm," Sabrina shook her arm in an attempt to free it from the woman's grip.

Instead, Marilyn's fingers pressed even harder into her
limb. "I will not allow you to go up there and say something to embarrass my family. We have dealt with enough
because of you."

"He's my father. He invited me here, and—"

Marilyn released her, almost violently. "And that was
bad enough. It's bad enough that I can never be rid of you.
But there are important people here. I do not want my
husband embarrassed and ridiculed for one stupid mistake in his past."

One stupid mistake... Sabrina swallowed, but the painful lump that had lodged in her throat would not go away.
"I am not a dirty little secret." She didn't appreciate the
way Marilyn was speaking to her. "People know about me.

They know of my father's *mistake* and forgave him when he came clean almost twenty years ago. If I'm here, why can't I celebrate my father like everyone else?"

"Be grateful you're here. Leave it at that. My children are upset. They look around, and you're here, and just think about how they feel. For God's sake."

Sabrina knew she shouldn't have come. But she didn't deserve to be belittled by Marilyn.

The bathroom door opened, and Julia stormed in. "What's going on here?"

Sabrina looked beyond Marilyn to Julia, holding out hope that Julia would not be as nasty as her mother had been. But Julia gave her a look of confused anger.

"All I wanted to do was speak about our—" Sabrina started, but Julia cut her off.

"Did you come here to cause trouble?" Julia asked. "Is that why you showed up?"

"Me? I'm not the one who's causing trouble. Your mother grabbed me. You saw—"

Sabrina didn't get to finish her statement, because Marilyn cried out. "Do you have any idea how this grieves my heart? Do you care?"

Julia instantly went to her mother's side and wrapped her arms around her.

"Of course." Sabrina exhaled sharply.

Clearly their argument had drawn attention, because the restroom door opened again, and two people Sabrina didn't know appeared. "What's going on?" a woman—who looked a lot like Marilyn—asked.

Marilyn dabbed at her eyes. "All I wanted was a nice evening to celebrate Gerald's birthday."

Sabrina wanted to say something, but knew that in this scenario, it was a losing battle. "Fine. Blame me. I'll leave."

She walked toward the restroom door, and the two women standing there parted so she could pass. That's when Sabrina saw that a couple of other people had congregated in the hallway, like gawkers at the scene of a car wreck. She quickly walked past them, noting their looks of disapproval.

And then she saw her father, standing at the end of the hallway that opened to the restaurant at large. He even looked disappointed in her.

"Sabrina, what happened?" he asked.

Why couldn't she hate him? It would be so much easier. He had never truly stood up to his wife from what she could tell, which had added to her misery over the years.

"Why don't you ask your wife?" Sabrina snapped. "But you won't, will you? You're happy to blame me for all of your problems."

She stormed past her father, and there was Mason. A sob escaping her, Sabrina rushed to him like a drowning person reaching for a buoy. Throwing her arms around his waist, she burst into tears.

Chapter 13

"Babe," Mason said, wrapping Sabrina tightly in his strong arms.

She clung to him and tried her best to even her breathing, but she was undeniably an emotional mess.

Sabrina wished she could hold back her tears. The last thing she wanted was for Marilyn to have the last laugh by seeing her in despair.

Why did I come here? she asked herself.

"What did your father's wife say to you?" Mason asked.

"Don't worry about it."

"I think this needs to be addressed."

"I just want to go," Sabrina said, looking up at him. She knew that right now, all eyes were on her, and she no longer wanted to give them a show.

"If that's what you want," Mason said.

"It is." She turned in his arms so that they could walk side by side, avoiding eye contact with the other guests. She held him as he went to their table so that Sabrina could retrieve her purse. Finally, as they neared the front door, the jazz musicians began to play again, a lively number that was sure to mask the sudden tension in the room.

"Do you want me to get your father so you can say goodbye to him?" Mason said once they were outside.

"Definitely not." When Sabrina realized that her voice had raised an octave, she gulped in air and tried to calm herself. She felt the tears stinging her eyes again, and she didn't want to break down on the street. She looked up at Mason, pleading. "You have the ticket for the valet?"

"Of course." He reached inside his blazer and found the ticket in his pocket.

"Will you meet me at the end of the street? I don't want to wait out here."

"No," Mason said, his eyes narrowing. "I won't. I'm not just going to let you just wander off."

"Please, just get me at the corner," Sabrina said, realizing that she sounded almost desperate. The last thing she wanted was for one of her so-called siblings or Marilyn or even her father to come out and give her more grief.

"Okay," Mason said, resigned.

Sabrina nodded, and then started to walk down the street as Mason went to the valet. When she was several feet away, she glanced over her shoulder and saw him staring after her in concern.

She turned and kept walking, wondering how she could have been so foolish to believe that coming there tonight was a good idea. Gerald might be her father, but trying to have a relationship with him was too painful. If he never stood up to his wife, how could Sabrina ever have a true relationship with him?

Sabrina stood at the corner and waited, wondering if all was back to normal in the restaurant. Perhaps Marilyn finally had a big grin on her face, elated that she'd been able to send her running.

Sabrina knew she had given the woman exactly what she'd wanted, but how could she do anything else when her father wasn't in her corner?

Mason pulled up to the curb. Ever the gentleman, he exited his Mercedes and rounded the car, heading toward her.

But Sabrina quickly moved forward, approaching the car door and opening it for herself. She slipped inside before Mason could reach her.

The look on his face said he was confused. But he said nothing as he closed the door and went back around to the driver's side of the car.

He got behind the wheel, saying, "Sabrina—"

"I don't want to talk."

"Don't shut me out."

She said nothing, just leaned her head back against the headrest and closed her eyes. After Mason had been driving for about a minute, he said, "You're not going to tell me what happened? One minute, you were going up to speak. The next minute, your father's wife dragged you off. I couldn't hear what was being said, but the entire restaurant knew something was up. And look at you…you're so upset, your hands are trembling. I don't know what's going on, but your father's wife doesn't have a right to be rude to you."

"No, she doesn't. But that doesn't stop her. She hates me. They all do."

"People get remarried all the time. There's no reason to hate you."

"It's not a normal divorce-remarrying situation," Sabrina said, and blew out a frazzled breath. "I'm my father's *bastard child*." Finally facing Mason, she gave him a poignant look for several seconds. "My father's been married to Marilyn for forty years, I think. But at some point, he met my mother. He and my mother had an affair. I was conceived. Marilyn forgave him, stayed with him. But every time she sees me, I guess all she can think about is the fact that my father strayed. She's never going to like me, let alone treat me with any decency. I've tried."

A few beats passed, and Mason said nothing. Then he said, "Now I understand. And that sucks. Really sucks. I'm sorry."

Sabrina shrugged. "What can you do?"

"But still, that was a long time ago. If your father's wife forgave him, what's the point in still being bitter?"

"She wants nothing to do with me, and can't even be civil. My half brother and sister are no better. I'm not sure why I even went to the birthday celebration. My father asked me to go, and Nya told me that I shouldn't let anyone keep me from being there for my dad." Sabrina swallowed painfully, wishing she had trusted her gut. "My God, could I feel any worse right now?"

Mason reached across the car and took her hand in his. "If they can't take the time to get to know you, it's their loss. Not yours."

"That's easy to say."

"It's also the truth."

Sabrina's gaze went to the right, looking out the window. The palm trees on Main Street were adorned with strings of clear lights wrapped around their trunks, a spectacular sight. On another night, Sabrina might appreciate the romantic setting. But tonight she simply felt angst.

Mason's words of comfort bothered her because it was what people always said. *It's their loss, not yours.* Those easy words didn't make her feel better about her life. Not that she expected Mason or anyone else to understand what she was going through. Being the child conceived of an affair was complex.

"Maybe we can get a drink somewhere?" Mason suggested. "At the marina, perhaps?"

"Actually, I just want to go home."

Mason said nothing. But a quick look at him told Sabrina that he was disappointed.

"I know you're upset, but you shouldn't let them ruin the rest of your night."

"Again, that's easy for you to say. I'm betting you have no clue what it's like to have family members who hate you."

"Is it a war zone when I'm at a family event?" Mason paused. "Not necessarily. But that doesn't mean I have the perfect family. Far from it."

"I'd take that over what I've got. I'm sure your family is not like the people we just left. Marilyn wouldn't be able to talk that way to me if my father did something about it. He wants me around, to act as though everything is all fine and dandy. But it's like he wants to have his cake and eat it, too. I think he lets Marilyn push him around because he feels guilty about what he did, but at some point he's got to take a stand.

"My mother isn't a threat to their relationship anymore. I'm the child in this, the innocent victim. I didn't ask to be born. My father needs to put Marilyn in her place and make sure that she doesn't treat me the way she just did ever again. I think if he spoke to my siblings, they would reach out to me. Welcome a relationship."

Suddenly, Mason pulled the car to a stop. And before Sabrina knew was happening, he was reaching for her and framing her face. "This really hurts, doesn't it?" he asked softly.

"Yes," Sabrina admitted, wishing that it didn't hurt as much as it did. "Aside from my mother, they're the only family I have. I wish it didn't matter to me, I wish I could just be as cold as they are. But all I keep thinking is that they're all I have. If something happens to my mother, then I'm all alone. I don't care that my father wasn't perfect. I'd just like to forge a relationship with my siblings."

Mason stroked her face with the pads of his thumbs. "Give it time," he said softly.

"I've given it time. Years."

"Then give it more time. You never know. One day they might just come around."

Sabrina glanced away, but Mason used his fingers to gently force her to face him again. "At least they're here.

They're breathing. They're alive. Trust me when I say this, some things don't get a second chance. And that's what really kills you."

Sabrina's lips parted as she looked at Mason. She then realized how insensitive she was being, especially with him. Yes, this situation had hurt. But at least her family was alive and well. With death, there were no second chances.

"I'm sorry," she said. "You must think I'm completely selfish."

"You just went through something awful. Obviously, you're going to feel upset about that. I'm just trying to let you see the light at the end of the tunnel."

"And I appreciate it," she said. "I just…I guess I just remembered how small my problems are compared to other people's. You lost the people you loved to tragedy. I can't even begin to know what that kind of pain is like."

Mason eased back and shifted in his seat, a look of discomfort on his face. "You asked me if I ever regret leaving the NBA. What happened to my mother and brother is why I don't. In a way, I became a firefighter in their honor. Sometimes when I rush into a burning building, it feels like I'm stepping back in time, wishing it could be the fire that consumed my house twenty years ago. That I've been given a chance to save my family."

Sabrina took her hand in his. "Oh, Mason."

"So, yes, I know a thing or two about when there is absolutely no hope, versus when there is. You showed up at your father's birthday celebration today, and that took guts. Who knows how your brother and sister are feeling about it. Maybe one day they'll reach out to you. Maybe they won't. But you can only do what you need to do, and if they don't come around, that's on them."

Suddenly, he was stroking her face. And Sabrina saw a man who was far more complex than she had ever imagined. His own heartbreak could surely be weighing heavily on his heart right now, and yet he comforted her.

"I'm glad you invited me," he said.

"It's not like we got to enjoy it."

"But I was able to be there for you." He paused, held her gaze. "And I don't want the night to end on a sour note. You're upset, and I'd like to do something to put a smile on your face."

She had shut him down when he had first suggested going to the marina. Now, as she looked at him, the ugly scene at the birthday party was fading from her mind. And all she saw was the incredible man she wanted to spend more time with.

"I'm not sure I'll be good com—"

Mason silenced her with a kiss. Sabrina was so startled that at first her eyes widened when his lips touched hers. She was too stunned to even react. But as his lips continued to move gently and seductively over hers, Sabrina released a small sigh. And when Mason drew her bottom lip between his and suckled softly, Sabrina's eyelids fluttered shut.

The sensations that overcame her were overpowering. She hadn't felt this kind of heat in a long time. This kiss was different than the others. There was intensity. A purpose.

And that purpose was seduction.

Snaking her arms around his neck, Sabrina surrendered to the kiss. She allowed herself to be consumed by the fire. Mason's fingers stroked her face and his tongue delved into her mouth.

Such sweet heat. Her need for this man was suddenly all consuming.

His hand went into her hair, pulling at the clip that held it in a bun. As he loosened her hair around her shoulders, he kissed the corner of her mouth, then her jawline.

The tip of his tongue then trailed to the underside of her jaw, and Sabrina felt a zap of explosive sensation in her sweet spot.

She gripped his shoulders and her mouth sought his hungrily. Oh, yes. Those full, delectable lips. The feel of his strong arms and shoulders. There wasn't an ounce of resistance left in her.

She wanted him.

But as her desire reached a fever pitch, Mason suddenly pulled away from her. Sabrina looked up at him through narrowed eyes, her chest heaving with each quickened breath.

"You know how beautiful you are?" Mason whispered. "I love looking at you. And that expression on your face now, the confusion…the lust—"

Sabrina actually chuckled. "Lust?"

"I see it. And I know what you're thinking right now."

Her body throbbed again. "What am I thinking?"

"You're thinking the same thing I'm thinking."

"And what are we thinking?"

Mason eased back, emitting a little groan as he looked toward his lap. "I think the cool air will do me some good."

"Wh-what?"

Mason opened the car door, leaving Sabrina hot, bothered and confused. Why wasn't he driving to her place?

Coming around to her side of the car, Mason opened the door and reached for her hand. "Why don't we go for a walk?"

Mason's level of lust was an eleven out of ten. If he didn't get out of the car, and quickly, he might not be able to control what happened behind the tinted windows.

"You want to go for a walk?" Sabrina asked.

He knew she was confused. One minute, they'd been

hurtling toward sexual action. The next, he was slowing things down.

"Sure," he told her. "We can head to the waterfront. It's not far."

"B-but...I'm not wearing proper shoes for walking."

"Then I'll carry you," Mason told her with a grin. "You know I have no problem with that."

Sabrina looked unsure. But finally said, "Okay. Let's go for a walk."

Mason took her hand and they strolled to the corner, turning right onto State Street. Live music was blaring through the open windows of a restaurant that offered nightly entertainment. Mason had been there several times, and enjoyed the various artists who played lively New Orleans' style jazz. If he didn't want to spend some quiet time with Sabrina, he would've suggested that they go there.

Instead, they walked the few blocks down to the stretch of waterfront where there were a host of shops and restaurants. Hand in hand, in silence. Just quietly enjoying each other's company.

As much as Mason had wanted nothing more than to drive to his place or Sabrina's and get naked, he'd known that he had to cool things down. No matter how intense his desire for her was, he didn't want to take advantage of her. Not while she was vulnerable and hurting.

"Beautiful night, isn't it?" Mason asked, coming to stop in front of a portion of the bay where sea lions liked to come and perch on the rocks. The moon was full, and its rays glistened like gold on the rippling waves.

"Yes, it is."

"You feel like getting a drink or something?"

"No." Sabrina shook her head, and then looked up at him. "Thank you for being here for me tonight. You seem to have known just what I needed. This walk...it's been peaceful, and it's helped calm my mind."

"Good. That's what I'd hoped for."

Sabrina offered him a slight smile. Mason wasn't sure why, but every time she smiled at him, something tugged on his heart. He wanted to wrap her in his arms and make all of her pain go away.

"I feel a little silly," she went on. "The way I fell apart in the restaurant. Then clung to you like I did. That's not usually how I behave."

"Let me guess. You're always strong. You don't need anyone."

"Sound like criticism…"

"It's not a criticism, it's an observation. But what I learned about you tonight explains a lot."

Sabrina looked out at the dark ocean. "I know when I went to the burn center with you, I said I would never complain about anything again. That the trials in my life simply aren't as great as those that other people face. Realistically, I know that. But on a night like tonight… It's hard to keep that perspective."

"Hey," Mason said softly. Standing behind her, he put both of his hands on her shoulders and gently rubbed. "It's okay to be upset. How can it be easy to live through the circumstances you've had to live through? Just because your issues are different from those who've gone through major tragedy, doesn't mean your pain don't hurt, too."

Sabrina turned in his arms, and looked up at him with what appeared to be wonder in her eyes. "Thank you for that. I don't believe in wallowing. That's not what I'm about. But you're right. Each of us has our own issues to deal with, and mine cut deep. It hurts knowing that your father won't stand up for you. But, he never did. So why am I even surprised?"

Mason saw the hint of pain in Sabrina's face, and hated that her family had caused it. He pulled her against his chest and cradled her head as he held her there. She clung to him, making a soft sound as she did. Was she crying?

"I'm sorry," she said after a long moment. "I don't know why I'm so emotional tonight."

"Don't apologize." Mason was happy that Sabrina allowed herself to be vulnerable with him. He sensed that it was something she didn't do too often.

She eased back and looked up at him, offering him a slight smile. And yes, there were tears. He brushed them away with the pads of his thumbs.

And then his thumbs stilled, and their eyes locked. He looked down at her, and she up at him. His heart began to speed up in his chest. He was beginning to feel that he had broken through the wall that Sabrina had erected to keep him and other men out.

"Why are you looking at me like that?" he asked.

"It's just…" She placed her palms on his chest. "It's just that you amaze me. I figured you for a hot guy with superficial wants and needs. But you're so much more than that. You have a giving heart, and a generous spirit."

Mason grinned, the words warming his heart. "Are you ready to admit that you like me?"

Sabrina didn't respond right away, but he saw something in her eyes.

"I do," she whispered.

He beamed. "Good. Because I definitely like you."

"How could you?" Sabrina asked. "I'm such a mess."

Slowly, he ran his fingers over both of her cheeks. "Trust me, there's a lot to like."

His fingers ventured closer to her mouth, and soon, he was smoothing his thumb over her bottom lip. Sabrina made a soft sound of delight.

"You're killing me," he said. "You know that, right?"

"No."

"Well, you are."

"Why's that?" she asked.

"You are so incredibly sexy. Even with tears in your eyes. There's something about you that just makes me feel…" He didn't finish his statement. "You're crying, and you're upset. And all I can think about is how beautiful your lips look in this lighting. How soft and delectable they were when I kissed you in the car." He paused. "I want so badly to kiss you again, when part of the reason I needed to get out of the car was so that I would stop kissing you."

"Why did you want to stop kissing me?"

"Because…I may be madly attracted to you, but I don't want to take advantage of the situation. You're hurting, and—"

"So you think I didn't really want to kiss you? I did so, to forget my pain?"

"Let's just say, I didn't want you making any decisions when your mind was clouded."

Sabrina said nothing, just turned her head to the side. Mason used his thumb to urge her face back toward him. He wasn't sure what she was thinking. "Did I say something wrong?"

She faced him again, and he felt her body shudder. "Exactly the opposite. You keep saying all the right things."

She wasn't just beautiful. There was something about her that made him want to protect her. Sabrina was different from the other woman he had dealt with in his past. Part of it was her feistiness. Her dogged resolve to do everything on her own. He wanted to see her weak with need.

Need for him.

"Are you too good to be true?" she asked.

"What you see is what you get."

She made a soft mewling sound, and Mason felt an instant sexual response. There was no doubt he wanted to make love to her.

"I want to kiss you so badly right now, it hurts. But I don't—"

"Want to take advantage of me?" Sabrina supplied.

Mason put both hands on her shoulders. "I want you to be willing. One hundred percent. Without anything clouding your judgment."

"Do you really think I'm not willing?" Holding his gaze, Sabrina eased forward and tilted her head back slightly, then parted her lips. "Do you honestly think I look distracted?"

For Mason, that was all the invitation he needed. He lowered his mouth onto hers, gently. Though what he felt was far from gentle. A raging desire began to consume him as his lips mated with hers.

She made another one of those soft, purringlike sounds, and damn if it wasn't the most beautiful thing he had ever heard. He deepened the kiss, moving his lips over hers with a bit more speed now. Placing a hand on her back, he drew her closer while slipping his tongue between her lips.

She quivered against him. And then she gripped his shoulder blades, arching up to kiss him back with fervor. He framed her face, held her in place as his tongue swept over hers with deep, broad strokes. It wasn't enough of her. He needed more.

While one hand stayed on her face, he returned the other hand to her back, smoothing it down her dress. For several seconds, he kept his hand respectably on her waist. But once she snaked her hand around his neck and flattened her breasts against his body, his hand went lower. Gripping her bottom, he pulled her tightly against him, knowing she would feel the evidence of his desire for her.

Now was the moment of truth. If she was frightened, she would pull away.

She pulled back. Mason's gut clenched. He was a gentleman. If she wanted to put a stop to things right now, he'd have to comply.

"I—" she began, then stopped. "I don't want to end this night alone."

A slow grin crept onto Mason's face. "Neither do I."

"My place?" she suggested.

Mason took her hand in his. "Let's go."

Chapter 14

Mason's lips held a slight smile as he looked down at her. Then, lifting their joined hands, he planted a kiss on hers.

Sabrina swallowed, wondering when her feelings for Mason had changed. It wasn't just that she wanted to get naked with him. But she truly *liked* him.

The fact that she wasn't scared to death about her sudden feelings spoke volumes. There was an intimacy between her and Mason, evidenced by the comfort of simply holding hands as they walked at a steady pace back to his car. It was an intimacy she was ready to take to the next level.

Once they reached the car, Sabrina felt a rush of excitement. Her heart was beating out of control. Her body was on fire. And she needed firefighter Mason Foley to come to her rescue…

Once they arrived at his Mercedes, Mason opened the passenger's door for her. But before she could get into the car, he drew her into his arms. Framing her face with one hand, he once again brought his lips down on hers. And right there, with people walking past them on the busy street, he kissed her as though he wanted the whole world to know she was his.

And she would be, at least for that night.

It was a skilled, delicious kiss, with gentle nibbles and flicks of his tongue. It was the kind of kiss that made Sabrina wish that they were already on her doorstep.

They got into his car, and the drive to her place seemed to take a lot longer than the usual ten minutes. Her breathing was shallow by the time they exited his car and headed to her door. As she slid the key into the lock, he came to stand behind her, resting his hands on her hips while his lips sought her neck.

Dropping her head backward, Sabrina exhaled a heavy breath as her eyes fluttered shut. She was looking forward to making love to Mason like she'd never looked forward to anything more in life.

"I can't get the door open with you distracting me," she rasped.

"Oh." His lips came off of her neck, but he continued to hold her waist. "Sorry."

Opening her eyes, Sabrina quickly unlocked the door. She walked up the stairs, and Mason followed behind her. She couldn't remember the last time she'd been particularly concerned about how well her clothes fit her body. But now, she hoped that, as Mason walked behind her, her behind looked decent in her dress.

"This," she said, opening the door to her apartment, "is my humble abode."

"Mmm," Mason said absently. He looped his arms around her waist. "Which way to the bedroom?"

"The open door on the right," Sabrina answered.

He spun her around and put his mouth on hers. Then, he began walking forward, causing Sabrina to walk backward. They moved that way until they crossed the threshold into her bedroom, their lips locked the entire way.

Once inside her room, the kiss intensified. Mason's hands roamed up her back with urgency. Sabrina pressed her body against his, needing to be closer to him.

His lips moved from her mouth to the underside of her neck, and she gripped his shoulders in response. Tilting her head back, she offered him more of her. He didn't dis-

appoint, burying his face in her neck and then gently suckling her sensitive skin. His tongue trailed a path of heat
from the base of her neck to just behind her ear and down
again. Then back up again, where he took her earlobe between his teeth and gently pulled, before softly suckling
the tender flesh.

"Oh, my God." Sabrina's knees buckled. The sweet sensations were simply overwhelming. She knew what she'd
told herself over and over again, that a casual affair was
not something she wanted. And yet, as Mason thrilled her
with his tongue, his lips and his teeth, all she wanted to
do was get naked and not worry if there would be a tomorrow for them.

Mason scooped her into his arms and carried her the
short distance to the bed. Once she was on her back, he
eased up so that he could look at her. Their eyes met and
held. Rays of moonlight flowed through the blinds, cast-
ing a romantic aura in the bedroom.

Sabrina reached for him, inviting him to lie with her.
But he didn't.

"What?" Sabrina asked, wondering if something was
wrong.

"I just want to look at you for a moment. Do you have
any idea how beautiful you are?"

A wave of euphoria washed over Sabrina. Hearing him
say that she was beautiful had a profound effect on her.
Here was this gorgeous man who could no doubt be with
anyone, and yet he was there with her. He was about to
make love to her.

Mason came down onto the bed beside her, and as his
lips found her neck, her head became light. Sabrina placed
a hand on his face, guiding it to her. And then she met his
mouth in a passionate kiss. She moved one hand around
his head, holding him in place as she pressed her body
against his.

With her other hand, she reached for his shirt and began pulling it from his pants. Once their breathing grew more intense, she used both hands to pull at his clothing. Mason slipped his fingers into her hair and kissed her hungrily as she concentrated on disrobing him. Gentle flicks of his tongue sent her thoughts tumbling, and she could hardly coordinate her fingers to get them to work properly.

Finally, he eased back. Smiling down at her, he removed his shirt. And although Sabrina had already seen him without his shirt on, she looked at the hard planes of his abs and rippling muscles in amazement. Because this time, she was appreciating him in a purely sexual way.

Mason took her hand and pulled her upward so that she was in a sitting position. Then he reached behind her to pull down her dress's zipper.

Mason is undressing me... Sabrina could hardly believe this moment was happening.

Gripping his forearms, she used him as leverage to get to her feet. Once standing, Mason's hands moved down her body to the hem of her dress. He pulled it upward and over her head, and then tossed it on the floor. His eyes held hers as his fingers went to her breasts. He trailed a finger over her heaping bosom, slowly, his eyes never leaving hers.

Standing there in her matching bra and panties, Sabrina had never felt more beautiful.

And then Mason kissed her again, a slow, tender, yet heat-filled kiss. As he did, he eased her backward on the bed once more, his own body coming down on top of hers. The feel of his bare skin on hers caused Sabrina to sigh from the pleasure.

Taking both of her hands in his, Mason extended them over her shoulders on the bed. Then he began to kiss a path from her lips down to the underside of her jaw, and down toward her breastbone. When he reached that spot, he released her hands. He then smoothed his hands over her

rib cage as his mouth also made its way down her body.
When he got to her navel, he softly kissed it, and then
dipped his tongue into the hollow space. Sabrina drew in
a sharp breath, her libido now in overdrive. It was obvious
that Mason was a man who knew how to please a woman.

He planted slow, delicious kisses along her belly. Then
his lips went lower, moving down one of her legs. When he
reached her knee, his lips moved to her inner thigh. With
deliberate slowness, he continued to kiss the inner part of
her leg, heading upward.

Sabrina's eyes fluttered shut. The anticipation was a
sweet sort of torture. When Mason's lips reached her belly
again, he slipped his fingers under the sides of her panties
and began to slowly pull them down.

Sabrina could not remember ever feeling this sexually
charged, and they were just beginning. Something about
the way Mason touched her made her feel absolutely incredible. Desirable in a way she had never seen herself.

With her panties off, Mason's hands went to her bra.
Then he slipped his fingers beneath the straps and pulled
them down. Sabrina eased up and reached behind her back
to undo the clasp, and the moment the bra loosened, Mason
stripped her of it completely.

Totally naked, Sabrina looked up at Mason. His playful
smile replaced with a look of wonder. It was as though he
was ensnared as his eyes roamed over her body.

Sabrina had never felt particularly comfortable being
naked, even in dim lighting. And after a few seconds of
Mason looking at her, she crossed her legs and covered
her breasts with her arm.

"Are you shy about being naked in front of me?" Mason
asked.

"I…" Sabrina couldn't think of what to say. On one
hand, the fact that Mason was staring at her naked body

was giving her a charge of sexual pleasure. On the other, she wasn't used to brazenly showing off her body.

"Don't worry," Mason rasped, and stroked her face. "I'm taking off my clothes off, too. And you can look all you like."

A thrill shot through Sabrina at his words, and then she watched as his hands went to his belt. He made quick work of stripping out of his pants and then his boxer briefs. Sabrina found herself lowering her arm from her breast as she watched his slow and sexy strip tease.

And when he stood before her without a stitch of clothing, Sabrina's breath caught in her chest. Seeing every inch of him was absolute perfection.

Mason stepped toward the bed. "I like how you look at me," he said. "What do you think?"

Sabrina blushed. Had she ever unabashedly stared at a naked man the way she was staring at Mason?

"Tell me," he encouraged her.

"I'm thinking that you're perfect. Every inch of you." She paused, and then reached for his thigh. She ran a fingertip up his strong leg, and was rewarded when she heard him groan. "And I'm thinking that I can't believe how lucky I am that you're here with me right now."

"I'm the lucky one," he said softly. "And you know what I'm thinking?"

Sabrina shook her head.

"I'm thinking that I can't wait to touch that beautiful body of yours all over. I want to make you sigh with pleasure. And I want to do it all night."

Sabrina's body shuddered as she thought of this gorgeous man pleasing her all night long. It was something she had never experienced, but she believed Mason could perform the task.

"I...I want that."

Mason got onto the bed beside Sabrina, framed her face

with both hands, and then began to kiss her. The kiss was deep and hot, and Sabrina moaned in protest when he tore his lips from hers. But then he dipped his head and kissed the mound of one of her breasts, and the moan of protest turned into a sigh of expectation.

His mouth went lower, and his tongue encircled her nipple. Hot tingles of pleasure spread from her breast throughout her entire body.

"Oh, yeah," Mason mumbled, and then he took her nipple fully into his mouth and suckled. He did it slowly and lovingly before increasing his speed and suckling her with fervor. Sabrina dug her fingers into shoulders, gripping him as he continued to work his mouth over her breast.

He then moved his mouth to her other breast. His lips and tongue tantalized her. He grazed her nipples with his teeth, tugged on them with his lips. Flicked them tenderly with his tongue.

Sabrina was so aroused, she could easily come.

Ending his delicious torture, he moved his mouth back to hers and kissed her as he stretched his body out beside hers once again. As he kissed her, his hands caressed her body. He smoothed his large flat palm over the underside of her neck and down toward her breastbone.

Balling her hands into fists, Sabrina began to writhe. And suddenly she realized that she was simply lying there, benefiting from his touches and kisses without doing the same to him. It had been so long since a man had touched her that she'd languished in the sensations.

Now, she put her hands on his skin and began running her fingers up and down his strong chest. Bringing one foot to the back of his leg, she began to rub it against his calf. She was still wearing her shoes, something she found incredibly hot. She felt like a sexy vixen.

"Ooh, yes," Mason moaned as Sabrina's hands went lower and around to his behind. "I love the way you touch me."

"I love how you feel," she told him.

"I want to give you the most pleasure you've ever experienced," he said. He then moved his mouth down her body, trailing kisses to her belly. Then moved his face to her upper thigh. He kissed the inside of it before positioning his mouth over her most feminine spot.

Sabrina held her breath. Mason began to gently stroke her with the tips of his fingers, causing the most heady and delicious sensations. And when he brought his mouth to her most sensitive place, Sabrina thought she would die from the pleasure.

Again, he was gentle and sweet and slow as he tantalized her. Even as Sabrina's body filled with raging sensations of lust, she couldn't help but feel that there was something magical and special about what was happening between them.

Suddenly she lost all train of thought as a climax so spectacular overcame her. "Mason!" she cried. "Oh, baby."

Mason continued to tease her body, drawing out her pleasure. She arched her back and gripped the sheets, loving every single moment.

Finally, her breathing began to subside, and she unclenched her fists. When she opened her eyes, she saw him looking at her. Smiling that charming smile. He skimmed her body with his hands as he kissed a delicate path up her belly, past her breasts, and to her mouth.

Wrapping her arms tightly around his neck, Sabrina kissed him deeply. If only this night could go on forever and ever.

"How was that?" he whispered.

"Amazing," Sabrina replied enthusiastically, her breathing still a bit ragged.

"Good." Mason kissed her cheek. "And that's just the beginning."

Rolling onto his back, he gently pulled Sabrina around

the waist onto his body. Though she was still lightheaded from her climax, she lowered her head and began to kiss his warm skin, slowly planting her lips over his chest.

She eased her body lower and reached for his shaft. Closing her hand around it, she grinned at him. My goodness, he was large and hard.

She stroked him, and Mason sighed. She stroked him again, and again, and felt a sense of power when his eyes closed. Then she added her lips, hoping that she was bringing him even half of the pleasure he had given her.

Mason trilled his fingers through her hair, and groaned as she teased him. Then, suddenly, he was urging her upward. His lips sought hers and he kissed her again.

"Gimme a quick second," he told her. Rolling over, he reached in the pocket of his discarded pants on the edge of the bed and withdrew a foil wrapper. He made quick work of putting on the condom, and then reached for Sabrina again.

She straddled him, and he guided his shaft into her.

They both moaned at the same time.

His hands went to her hips, holding her in place as he began to fill her, slowly, making sure he wasn't going too fast. Sabrina looked into his eyes as the glorious feelings intensified. She could hardly catch her breath.

And when he filled her completely, she cried out in pleasure.

"Yes," Mason rasped.

They began to move together, slowly, finding their rhythm. Mason continued to look at her. The expression of ecstasy on his face was as much a turn on for her as their physical sensations.

They quickened their pace. And with each stroke, Sabrina reached a place of tantalizing bliss.

Then she climaxed. This one more earth-shattering

than the first time. And as she cried out Mason's name,
she knew that she wanted more than one night with him.
   Much more.

Chapter 15

The next morning, Sabrina opened her eyes to see Mason lying beside her, resting on an elbow, and staring at her.

"Morning," he said.

"Morning," Sabrina replied, then blushed as she remembered the scandalous night they'd shared. "Gosh, what time is it?"

"After eleven."

Sabrina shot up. "Eleven!"

"Well," Mason said, a sheepish grin crawling onto his lips. "We were up most of the night."

Her head beginning to throb, Sabrina eased back down. "We certainly were."

"I told you I would please you all night."

"And you are most definitely a man of your word."

"Disappointed?"

"Disappointed?" Sabrina looked incredulous. "Absolutely not. I couldn't be more satisfied."

Mason stroked her cheek. "Good."

Sabrina eased up and planted a soft kiss on his lips, then snuggled close to him. "I know I should be a good host and get up and make you some breakfast, but you have to give me a minute."

"Actually, why don't you let me get you breakfast?" Mason asked. "If your fridge is stocked, I can prepare something."

Sabrina stared at him, saying nothing.

"Oh. Okay. You don't like anyone else running your kitchen?" he asked.

Sabrina realized he had misconstrued her silence. "No," she said. "That's not it. It's more like I'm not used to…"

"Being treated well?" Mason asked. "Yeah, I got that sense from you. I'm happy to be the one to spoil you. Breakfast is always the meal I prepare at the firehouse. Do you have eggs?"

"Yes."

"Potatoes?"

"Yes."

Mason got out of bed, stark naked. "Then you wait here while I make you breakfast. Though I think I'll take a shower first. Where's your bathroom?"

"Turn right out of the bedroom. It's the door at the far end of the hall."

Sabrina shamelessly checked out his incredibly gorgeous body as he walked out of her bedroom door. Before leaving, he looked over his shoulder and offered her a smile.

He was stunning to look at, and he'd been incredible in bed. But what tugged at Sabrina's heart was his kind nature. The fact that he was happy to get up and prepare her breakfast impressed her.

A couple of minutes later, she heard the shower going. How could she truly lie back and rest when Mason was naked in her shower?

Sabrina got out of bed, went down the hallway to her bathroom, and stepped inside. Mason had his face under the shower head, so he didn't see her coming.

Grinning, Sabrina pushed aside the shower curtain and stepped in behind him. Then she cupped one of his butt cheeks.

Mason jerked his head over his shoulder, and looked down at her in surprise. A smile crept onto his lips.

"I figured you might need some help washing your back," Sabrina said.

"Did you now?" Mason asked.

Sabrina smoothed her hands up his back. "Well, we did get very sweaty last night."

Mason turned to fully face her, and his wet body pressed against hers. "You're right about that."

As water sluiced over both of their bodies, Sabrina leaned forward to kiss Mason. Their kissing led to touching and to another round of making love.

Later, as Sabrina enjoyed a delectable breakfast of grilled potatoes and an omelet filled with vegetables, she looked at Mason across her kitchen table.

"About last night—" she started.

"Don't say it," Mason said. "Don't tell me that you think last night was a mistake—not while you're enjoying the breakfast I prepared for you."

Mason said the words with a smile, letting Sabrina know that he was joking. Although she wouldn't be surprised if he too, was uncertain about what their relationship was. "Actually, that's not what I was going to say at all. Far from it. I was going to say that I enjoyed last night. Not the part where I was a mess, but afterward."

"That's nice to hear." Mason winked at her. "I enjoyed spending time with you, too. And for the record, you were not a mess."

"I was," Sabrina insisted. "I got all emotional about my father and his family."

"It's not easy," Mason said. "I understand that, probably more than you know."

Sabrina raised an eyebrow as she looked at him. "Really?"

"I have a complicated and troubled relationship with my father, as well."

Now Sabrina was even more curious. "You do?"

Mason ate the last bit of his omelet before speaking. "My father has always had a problem with alcohol. He's what you'd call a functioning alcoholic. The problem is, you can't force someone into treatment."

Mason paused, and a look of torment came over his face. Sabrina reached for his hand. "Go on."

"The night my mother died, my father was out at a bar with some friends. Drinking, as usual. While my mother was home alone."

"What you mean your mother was home alone? Where were you?"

"I was at summer camp. My parents weren't getting along, and they fought all the time. Mostly about my dad's drinking, and how much he was spending on alcohol. And when he was drinking, he liked to hit the casinos and gamble, so that was a bone of contention between my parents, as well. I was old enough to understand that they had an unhappy marriage, and the fights…they were getting to me. I wanted to escape. I begged to go to a summer camp for two weeks, and when my parents agreed, I was so excited. Until the day one of the counselors came into my room one morning and told me what had happened."

Suddenly, Sabrina understood why he seemed to still feel significant pain over the loss of his mother and baby brother. Not just because he hadn't been there the night they'd died, but because he had opted to be away.

Gently, she squeezed his hand. "I get the sense that you blame yourself that you think that if you'd been there things would be different. But Mason, it's not your fault."

"I know things would have turned out differently had I been there. I was old enough. I would have smelled the smoke…I would have gotten my mother and brother out…"

"Oh, Mason." Sabrina's heart broke for him. "You really shouldn't blame yourself. You couldn't know what was going to happen."

"What kills me is that I wanted to get away so badly. I wanted to get away from their fighting. I got my wish, but I lost so much in return."

"No, don't say that. You were a child. You can't be responsible for the adult problems your parents were facing or for wanting to get away from being in the middle of it." She linked her fingers with his, and looked into his eyes. "I know your mother wouldn't want you feeling guilty about this all of these years."

"Maybe not."

"Definitely not. There's no way that she would. Everything that you've said about her shows me she was a caring and loving person. A wonderful mother." Sabrina paused. "I can't say I understand the gravity of your loss, but I do hope you can try to cherish the memories with your mother. And mostly, that you can forgive yourself."

Mason raised their joined hands and pressed his face against the back of her hand. Closing his eyes, he nodded. And for a long while, he didn't say anything.

"My father and I still aren't close," he said. "Not just because of that night, but because he still chooses the bottle over a relationship with me."

"I'm sorry," Sabrina said softly. Then, leaning close, she kissed him on the cheek. "I know it hurts."

She felt his warm breath as he exhaled heavily. Knowing he was reliving his pain, Sabrina stroked his cheek with her free hand. And then she slowly began to angle his face toward hers as she moved hers closer to his.

Her lips met his, in a soft, comforting kiss.

As he kissed her back with an almost sense of desperation, Sabrina knew she was falling.

Falling hard.

Sabrina looked back on the past few weeks with Mason. They had been spending as much time together as possible from going out to dinner to staying in watching movies. And despite everything Sabrina had told herself about guarding her heart, she knew that she was beyond simply falling in like with Mason.

She had fallen in love.

"So you're all set for New York," Nya said to her as she gathered her lunch bag from the fridge in the small kitchen at the end of the work day. "They apologized profusely for the mix-up and assured me they have your room for two nights."

"I knew you'd work it out," Sabrina said, jarred from her thoughts.

"How are you going to survive two days without Mason?" Nya asked as she started out of the kitchen.

"I'll be busy with the wedding," Sabrina said.

"But at night, when you're finished and alone in the bed…"

Sabrina followed Nya to the reception area. "Then it will make it that much sweeter when we see each other again."

Grinning at her, Nya went behind her desk. "I'm jealous. I mean, honestly, just looking at your face says it all. I've never seen you look this happy in…well, in forever."

"I am happy," Sabrina said, hardly believing the words coming from her mouth. "He's just…a great guy. I keep trying to find faults, but I can't."

"And I'm sure the sex is off the charts." Nya wriggled her eyebrows.

Sabrina blushed as she sat against the edge of Nya's desk. "It *is* pretty amazing."

"Girrrl, that's what I'm talking about!"

"But, I don't know," Sabrina said, standing up from the desk. "I mean, things are great now. But long-term?"

"Take it one day at a time. Don't stress about tomorrow." Nya picked up her purse from the floor behind the desk. "And wish me luck on my date tonight."

Sabrina crossed fingers on both of her hands. "Fingers crossed," she said, raising them. "And I like what you're wearing." Nya's outfit of a knee-length black skirt and pink blouse did not scream SEX for once.

"I'm taking your advice," Nya said.

"Hope this guy ends up being a nice one."

"Me, too. I am so ready for a real relationship!"

Sabrina and Nya hugged. "And you deserve that."

They pulled apart, and Nya headed to the door. "See you tomorrow," Nya said.

"Have fun."

As Nya exited the building, Sabrina's mind went to Mason as it did so often now, wondering what he was up to. She hadn't seen him yesterday, because he'd been working, and today he was doing firefighter training with some new recruits.

She went to her office, retrieved her cell and sent Mason a message asking him about his day. Then she got to work on some of the photos of a new baby. Living right upstairs, she often stayed in her office longer than business hours.

Half an hour later, her cell phone made the whistling sound that indicated she had a text message. She quickly scooped up the phone and looked to see who had contacted her.

When she saw the message from Mason, she beamed.

Are you in your studio? I want to drop by.

Sabrina quickly texted the reply: I'm here.

Ten minutes later, she heard the door chimes singing. Her stomach fluttered with a mix of excitement and nervousness, knowing that Mason had arrived. After being so long since she'd been involved with anyone, it was a sweet and welcomed feeling.

She got up from her desk and wandered to the hallway, where he greeted her outside her office door. Instantly, a smile spread across his face. "Hey, beautiful."

Sabrina would never tire of hearing him address her that way. "Hey."

Stepping toward her, Mason pulled her into his arms and began to kiss her. Sabrina's head grew light, and the work she'd been doing was instantly forgotten.

Releasing her, Mason strolled into her studio. He walked up to the backdrop where she had done her last photo session. And when he turned to face her, she saw that he had started to unbutton his shirt.

"What are you doing?" Sabrina asked.

A devious smile playing on his lips, Mason continued undoing the row of buttons.

Sabrina knew that they were alone in her studio, yet she threw a glance over her shoulder nonetheless.

"You know nobody's coming in here."

"Why are you taking your shirt off?" And why here, in front of the backdrop? They could just as easily head upstairs to her bedroom.

"You've got the camera set up. And you've got a willing model. Let's have a little fun."

"What kind of fun?" Sabrina asked, looking at him through narrowed eyes.

"As much as you want."

Sabrina began to chuckle. "You want me to take pictures of you with your shirt off?"

"For a start." He shrugged out of his shirt and threw it onto the floor. "And whatever else you'd like," he added with a naughty grin.

Sabrina swallowed. Her eyes roamed over his magnificent upper body. The hard grooves and planes of his stomach and his eight-pack abs. The ridges of muscles in his arms and his broad shoulders.

She wanted to put her tongue on him.

"Come on," Mason urged her. "Let's get a little risqué…"

Chapter 16

Let's get risqué... Had anything sounded more provocative?

"You're serious?"

"As a heart attack."

Sabrina could hardly think, as images of him naked entered her mind. She couldn't imagine a day when she would tire of seeing him naked.

"What are you waiting for?" Mason asked. "You don't think I'll make a good model?"

"Give me a second." She scooted out of the studio and went to the front door and locked it. Then she went back to the studio and stood behind her camera, which was set up on the tripod.

"Okay." Sabrina tried to speak as professionally as possible. "Let's take some photos."

Mason angled his body posing for her. "Ooh, that's good." Then she giggled as he made a silly face. "That's it, work it."

He continued to try a variety of poses, like a pro. Whether serious or silly in the poses, the shots looked great. Sabrina laughed, enjoying the spontaneous and fun interlude.

"I hate that you're going to New York."

"What?" Sabrina said, caught off guard by the unexpected comment.

"Two days away from me…" He flexed his muscles. "How do you feel about company?"

"You…you want to go to New York with me?"

"Why not?" he asked. "I think it'd be fun. You leave on Friday, and I work that day. But I could head to New York first thing Saturday morning after my shift."

Sabrina's fingers stilled on the camera. "But it's not like I'm going for a vacation. I'll be working. And my flight back to California is Sunday morning."

Mason shrugged and began to pose again. "Just a thought. You could always change your flight… Spend Sunday with me there."

"Or, I could just come back to Ocean City and see you here."

Mason said nothing, just continued to pose, and Sabrina started clicking the shutter button again. After about a minute, Mason asked, "Where's that stuff you've got?" Mason asked. "The stuff you use to grease down men's bodies?"

"You want me to use some of that on you?"

"Of course. Let's make this as legit as it can be."

"Okay." Sabrina went off to the shelf where she had her special concoction, then made her way over to Mason. He looked down at her with expectation as she began to spray his torso with the oil and water mixture.

"Make sure you rub it in now," Mason told her, his voice a little husky.

Sabrina put her left hand on his chest. But instead of rubbing in the concoction, she let her hand rest there, feeling the heat from his skin against her palm. They had been naked together a number of times now, but she never tired of touching his body. Slowly, she moved her hands over his torso, making sure to spread the baby oil and water mixture evenly.

"That's right," Mason said. "Make sure you put it all over."

He turned around, and she began to work her palms over his back the way she had done with other clients before. She had always been able to apply the mixture to her clients with a completely professional attitude. But now, her thoughts were undeniably *unprofessional.* All she could think about was stroking Mason in a way that would have him taking her in his arms and heading upstairs with her.

Slowly, Mason turned around again. And when he looked down at her, Sabrina's breath caught in her throat. Was he ready to be done with this game and take her to bed?

"All right. I think I'm ready for some more pictures."

"You are." Sabrina's voice sounded like a croak. Though her body was thrumming with lust, she made her way back behind the camera and took more pictures. And when Mason unbuttoned his jeans, her mouth literally watered.

Mason's eyes held hers as he dragged his jeans over his hips. As he moved them down his legs, Sabrina began snapping more photos. Standing in front of her in only his briefs, he continued to pose, a look of longing in his eyes.

Mason turned around, exposing his back. And as he did, he pushed his briefs slowly over his buttocks, revealing his tight behind. Not all of it, but enough. Enough for her to want to step away from the camera and start taking off her own clothes.

"How's that?" he asked, angling his head over his shoulder to look at her.

"It's fabulous."

"Are you still taking pictures?"

Sabrina snapped some shots. "Yes."

Mason then bent over as he worked the briefs off of his body, and Sabrina drew in a sharp breath. Mason still didn't turn to face her, and Sabrina was fine with that. She didn't mind drinking in the sight of his tantalizing behind.

Mason flexed his arms, displaying his muscular and

magnificent back. Sabrina's body was ripe with sexual need, but she forced herself to take more pictures of him. Stark naked from the behind, she wanted him to turn around. And she was itching to go over to him and plant her lips on his hard chest.

Again, Mason angled his head to the side and looked at her. "Are you ready? This is the grand finale."

"I'm ready," she told him, her voice raspy.

Slowly, Mason turned. She had expected him to perhaps cover himself first, but he didn't. He turned, exposing every inch of his beautiful manhood.

Sabrina was almost too shocked to take any photos. She stood and stared at his body that had given her worlds of pleasure.

She couldn't wait any longer.

"Aren't you taking any more pictures?" Mason asked.

But Sabrina was already stepping away from the camera and walking toward him. Her eyes locked with his as she approached. And as she reached him and placed her hands on his chest, she heard and felt the rumble emanate from it. She smoothed her hands up his chest and onto his broad shoulders and rose up onto her toes. Mason lowered himself and brought his mouth onto hers.

Their lips came together in a fireball of passion. Hot and frenzied. Their tongues mated with each other's with a need as old as time. Mason's hands tightened around her waist and he lifted her easily. Sabrina purred and gripped his shoulders tighter while wrapping her legs around his waist.

She was on fire. But the fire that consumed her was one that she didn't want to be put out. She wanted to let it burn, let her all-encompassing need for this gorgeous man totally consume her.

Mason slipped his hands beneath her dress, running them up her legs until he reached her behind. He gripped her bottom and deepened the kiss. Sabrina dug her fingers into his skin. Mason began to ease their bodies down, and Sabrina lowered her legs to the floor to help with the balance. As soon as she was stable, Mason's hands reached for the buttons on the front of her dress. He worked quickly and efficiently, undoing them and then pushing the fabric away from her breasts and over her shoulders.

"Oh, yes," he uttered, before cupping her breasts. Even with her bra on, the heat intensified. Her nipples began to ache as they hardened. And the only thing that could assuage the ache was Mason.

His fingers. His lips.

"We could be doing this in New York," Mason said. "Think about it…"

"I'll be busy with the wedding," she said, but the truth was, she didn't want to think about New York. Her mind was on now.

"And at night, I could rock your world."

As if to prove his point, Mason brought one of his hands to her neck and smoothed his palm over her skin. Then he went lower, to the area between her breasts. Sabrina fiddled with the clasp of her bra behind her back until she undid it. With her bra loosened, Mason pulled the straps down her arms, freeing her of the garment. Sliding one hand around to her back, he held her firmly in place as he brought his mouth onto one nipple, hungrily drawing it into his moist, warm mouth.

Sabrina cried out in ecstasy. Every touch was magnificent. He suckled her nipple with fervor, making her feel light-headed from the delightful sensations. Never in her life had anyone made her feel this incredible.

Mason's mouth moved to her other breast, where his tongue twirled around that nipple before he fully drew it into his mouth. This time, he suckled softly, which heightened her pleasure even more. Sabrina made a mewling sound of delight, and stroked Mason's face.

"Yes, baby," she whispered.

One of Mason's hands went beneath her dress in search of her most sensitive spot. And when he found it, he began to gently stroke her as he continued his soft suckling. Sabrina's eyes fluttered shut as the sensations began to build, like a wave heading to the shoreline. And when Mason grazed her nipples with his teeth while stroking her nub, she shattered.

Mason's fingers and tongue didn't relent, drawing out her pleasure until she was whimpering his name. Spent from her climax, Mason eased her onto the floor. Then he fully removed her dress from her body as well as her panties. And though she had a bed upstairs, it was too far away. Sabrina wanted this man and wanted him now.

And he wanted the same thing, because he got a condom from his pants' pocket and put it on. Then he lowered himself onto the floor beside her and began to kiss her. The entire world melted away, and all she wanted was to spend the rest of her life naked with this man.

Their lips locked, Mason pulled her onto his hard body. Looking down at him, Sabrina was surprised by the desire to whisper those three little words. But she couldn't say them. Not yet. She only hoped that Mason understood how much what they were doing meant to her.

He smiled at her, the kind of content, desire-filled smile that made her feel all feminine. But the smile quickly disappeared as he moved a hand around the back of her neck and pulled her mouth down onto his. He kissed her again, ferociously, as though he couldn't get enough of her. And as he did, his other hand guided his shaft inside of her. He did it with gentle skill, easing his way in, and still sexily kissing her until he filled her completely.

Nothing had ever felt this good. Each time they were

together was more exciting than the last, which Sabrina didn't think was possible. She arched her back and rode him, knowing that each stroke that filled her was about much more than the act of having sex.

She opened her eyes and looked down at him, and saw him looking up at her.

"You're so beautiful," he told her.

Those words were like an aphrodisiac. Both physical and emotional. Mason was a wonder to her.

As their bodies moved together, giving and receiving pleasure, Sabrina felt her climax begin to build.

"That's it, baby," Mason whispered. "Oh, yes. I'm there, too."

"You are?" Sabrina asked on a moan.

"Yes…"

Sabrina held his gaze as her climax claimed her. A second later, Mason's also claimed him. Together they were consumed by passion's flame. And in Sabrina's mind, there was nothing more beautiful.

Spent from her orgasm, she collapsed on top of him. Her erratic heartbeat pounded against his slick chest. And she could feel his fast heartbeat thumping against her body. She wanted to lie on top of him, their moist bodies joined forever.

She had never felt more alive in her life. Never more a woman.

"How's your back?" she asked.

"I'm o—"

Before Mason could finish his statement, there was a loud crash. It took Sabrina's brain a moment to realize that the crash had been the sound of a window breaking.

The front of her store!

Mason was already easing her off of him, and quickly grabbing his pants. But he didn't put them on right then, instead he quickly covered himself and started for the front door of her studio.

"Mason!" Sabrina called.

But he had already charged out the door and toward the front of her office.

Chapter 17

Sabrina quickly slipped into her dress and hurried out to the front of the shop to meet Mason. As she got closer, she saw the broken glass everywhere. The largest front window had been smashed in.

"No!" she exclaimed.

Mason looked over his shoulder at her. "Someone threw this rock through your window." He held up a fairly large rock to show her what had caused the damage. "But by the time I got out here, I didn't see anyone."

"Mason, go back into my studio and put your clothes on." He was covering the front of his body with his jeans, but his behind was completely exposed. From her vantage point, it was okay, but anyone walking by and peering would realize the sexual nature of what had been going on.

Mason nodded, understanding. "Right. Okay."

Mason backed up, to keep his butt from being exposed to anyone on the street, until he got the door that led into her studio. Only then did Sabrina check out the damage, her eyes going from the large, gaping hole in the window to the shards of glass on the floor.

She stifled a cry. Who would do this? And why?

Less than a minute later, Mason was back at her side. He was wearing his shirt and had his jeans pulled on, but not zipped up.

"I can't believe this," Sabrina said, facing the scene of vandalism.

"Do you have any idea who would do this?" Mason asked.

"No." Sabrina groaned. "I'm going to have to tape up this window and have it replaced tomorrow."

Sabrina started to walk forward, but Mason scooped her around her waist and pulled her back. "Be careful of your feet."

"You, too," she said.

"Too late," he said.

Sabrina whirled around. Mason raised his left foot, and she instantly saw blood. "Mason!"

"I'm okay," he told her. "But there's blood on your floors. I got the shard out, so I'm good."

"Baby." Sabrina slipped her arms around his waist.

"Don't worry about me. I'm more concerned about you, and who would do this. I'm just glad I was here when this happened."

Sabrina squeezed him tightly. "I'm glad you're here, too." She would have been frantic if this had happened while she was there alone. "Why don't you go back into my studio and take a seat. I've got Band-Aids in the bathroom."

"My foot can wait until you call the police."

"I'm sure it can, but I'm going to get a bandage for it nonetheless. Then I'll call the police."

Mason took a seat behind Nya's desk. "How about I call the police while you get the Band-Aid?"

Sabrina nodded. "All right. But I'm sure it was just kids causing trouble."

"But you can't be sure of that," Mason insisted. "The cops need to be called. They need to come and examine the scene."

"You're right. Okay, you call the while I get the bandage."

She headed off to the bathroom. She knew Mason wasn't critically injured, but she wanted to take care of him nonetheless.

Mason stayed with Sabrina as the police came and took their statements and examined the scene. He was glad that he knew both of the cops who'd come to investigate. He would have no problem following up with them to see how the investigation was going.

If they actually investigated the vandalism. Because of the way Sabrina was suddenly downplaying the event with the officers, Mason had no clue if they would take the occurrence seriously.

"Honestly, I don't think anyone has targeted me," Sabrina said. "I don't have any customers who are upset with me. And you said yourself that there have been some random acts of vandalisms around the area."

"True," Officer Ramirez said. "But we shouldn't rule anything out."

"I'm a photographer," Sabrina went on. "People leave my studio happy."

"Understood," Officer Ramirez continued. "But sometimes, you never know. People are unpredictable."

"Not to mention that it could easily be a jealous competitor," Mason piped in. "That's something I'm familiar with from the cases of arson that are plaguing the city right now."

Sabrina shrugged, but the look on her face said that she wasn't convinced.

"All right," Officer Bramwell said, and closed his notebook. "I think we have all we need for now. Here's my card." He handed it to Sabrina. "Call if there's anything else you remember. And of course, if something else happens."

"I'm sure it won't." Sabrina folded her arms over her

chest and followed the cops to the door. "In fact, I feel a little silly having you come here. I mean, I'm sure it was a bored kid. And if so, I don't want to press charges."

"You were right to call," Officer Ramirez told her at the door.

"You need a police report for insurance purposes at the very least," Mason said, feeling a mix of annoyance and confusion. He couldn't understand how she hadn't thought of the obvious in terms of possible suspects. He hadn't thought it was his place to mention it before, but now as the officers were about to leave, he called out, "Wait a second." When both cops looked at him, Mason continued. "I just considered something. In terms of possible suspects, I think you should talk to some members of Sabrina's family."

Sabrina's head whipped around and she gaped at him.

"We were at Sabrina's father's birthday party. There was a heated exchange between Sabrina and her father's current wife. There's apparently long-standing animosity between her father's family and Sabrina. Sabrina can tell you about it."

"Oh?" Officer Bramwell opened up his notebook once more. "When was this party?"

"A couple of weeks ago," Sabrina answered.

"And what happened?" Officer Bramwell asked.

Sabrina sighed, and shot a glance at Mason. It was clear that she was more than uneasy. She was angry.

But she went on, telling the story of what had happened at the birthday party and the long standing animosity between her and her father's family.

"But," she added once she was done, "I can't imagine any of them doing anything like this."

"That's not unusual," Officer Ramirez said. "Sometimes, those closest to us hurt us in ways we wouldn't believe they were capable of. I'm not saying either of them are guilty, but this is a lead we'll definitely look into."

Mason was right about Sabrina being angry, because the moment the cops were gone, she faced him and said, "Why did you do that?"

"Why did I do what?"

"Why did you tell them about my father's family? Do you think I need any further problems with them? That I need to give them even more reason to despise me?"

"There's bad blood between you all," Mason said, not understanding why she didn't get it. "Obviously, they need to be considered as suspects. If the police are going to investigate this, they need to be able to investigate all angles."

"And if they had nothing to do with it, they're only going to hate me even more."

Mason stared at her, confused. "And? Seems they already hate you."

"My father," she said, sounding exasperated. "I'm trying to forge a good relationship with him, and this—accusing his family—will only cause more of a rift between us."

"You cried on my shoulder after your father's party, upset that he didn't come to your defense. If he's going to use this as further excuse not to be in your life, then shame on him. The way I see it, he needs to man up and stop walking the fence."

Sabrina threw her hands up and turned away from him, as if she couldn't stand to look at him any longer. "I want you to leave now."

"What?" Mason asked, stunned.

"I'm not in the mood to talk. Nor to be with anyone."

For a moment, he didn't know what to say. He didn't expect her to be so upset with him. "No," he finally said. "I don't want to leave."

Sabrina faced him, looking aghast. "Excuse me?"

"Someone threw a rock through your window. You could have been hurt. And on top of that, even if it was a kid behind this, your place is still vulnerable because of the broken window. I want you to come to my place."

Mason wasn't entirely sure why those words had come from his mouth. He had not lived with a woman in years. And the last one he'd lived with had left him a note while he'd been at work, explaining that she didn't think their relationship was going anywhere and that she couldn't continue to live in sin. Regardless, he wanted Sabrina at his place to make sure she was safe.

"I don't think you heard what I said."

She was mad, he got that. But surely she wouldn't put herself in harm's way just to make a point.

"You live above your studio. Your place was vandalized. Whether or not you want to think that someone with a vendetta was out to get you, it's something you should consider. And the fact that you're here practically all day... I'm sure some people are aware of that. I'm not saying it has to be someone from your father's family. But God only knows how many people you come into contact with. Maybe one of them had something to do with this."

"Like I told the police officers, I've never had an irate customer."

"And like they said, that doesn't mean anything," Mason persisted. "Some people are just crazy." He blew out a frazzled breath. "Just come to my place. Stay the night there."

She looked at him, her chin jutted out slightly. "I'll be fine here."

"Are you really that stubborn? I'm offering you somewhere safe to stay. And you're turning me down?"

"Since you haven't figured it out, I'm not happy with you right now."

"Because I mentioned some of your father's family should be considered as suspects?"

"Because you seem to not care about my feelings."

"Why—because you want me to pretend that some kid with nothing to do is behind this?" He gestured to the broken window.

"You don't understand," she said. "And I don't need you to take care of me. I've taken care of myself for years."

"Ahh, so that's what this is about? You're hell-bent on proving that you're a self-sufficient woman who doesn't need a man?"

"I'm done with this conversation. Can you please leave?"

Seeing the look of anger on her face, Mason knew there was no point pushing the issue. "Fine." He spun around and headed for the door. Opening it harder than was necessary, he stormed outside.

Once on the sidewalk, he drew in a breath to calm his frayed nerves. Then he looked over his shoulder, hoping to see Sabrina coming to the door.

She wasn't there.

Gritting his teeth, he walked over to his car and got inside. But he didn't drive away. He sat, his mind whirring, as he tried to figure out what had happened.

Why was she so upset with him? He was simply trying to help. Both with the investigation and with her living arrangements while her place was vulnerable. Yet she had gone from making love to him as though he was the only man who could pleasure her, to telling him to leave.

Mason didn't *want* to believe that her father's family could be so callous as to try and hurt her, but he'd been at the birthday party. He had witnessed how they'd treated her. The conflict had been ugly, the tension between them ripe. The way Mason saw it, one of them could easily be behind this. That's the only reason he brought it up with the police.

No one would be happier than him to learn that the culprit had simply been some teen looking for a laugh. But Mason didn't want to rest until there were clear answers.

Even though Sabrina had banished him from her place of business, Mason wanted to turn back around, pull her into his arms and kiss her until she saw reason. He'd never said that she wasn't capable of taking care of herself, but he wanted to be there for her.

In a way that surprised him. He wasn't used to being this worried about someone. Kenya had gone off all over the world, and texted or called him from various cities to tell him what was going on. Yet Mason had never been overly worried about her safety. But his gut clenched at the thought of something happening to Sabrina.

He looked over his shoulder in the direction of Sabrina's shop. He looked at the cardboard that he'd helped her tape over the broken portion of the window, thinking it wasn't nearly secure enough.

He was about to get out of his vehicle and march back to the shop when he saw the door open. Sabrina exited, locked the door and then looked in the direction of his vehicle. When she started to walk toward his car, Mason's stomach tightened.

She came around to the driver's-side door. A tentative smile forming on his face, Mason opened the door to greet her.

"Here," she said, extending her hand.

Mason looked at her palm. "What?"

"The SD card from the camera. I figure you'd feel more comfortable with it being in your possession."

Mason swallowed, uncomfortable. Then he took the SD card and said, "Sure. Thanks."

Without another word, Sabrina turned and started to walk away.

Irked, Mason shoved his key into the ignition and

started his car. Then he pulled away from the curb and into traffic faster than he planned to.

But no matter how fast he drove, he couldn't escape the thought plaguing him.

What the heck just happened?

Chapter 18

"Just so I'm clear," Nya said to her the next morning, her eyes narrowed with confusion and disappointment, "he wanted to protect you and you all but told him to go to hell?"

Sabrina sat on the chair in front of Nya's reception desk and bit at her bottom lip. "It's not that simple."

"Then explain it to me so that I can understand. Because from where I'm sitting, it seems you totally overreacted."

Sabrina pouted. "He never even considered the consequences of having the police go to my father's family and question them. He should have asked me before blurting it out."

"So this is about you still wanting to have a relationship with people who have made you feel like an outcast for how many years?"

Nya's question was blunt. And hearing it, Sabrina was forced to face reality. Softly she said, "Maybe it is."

Perhaps because Sabrina had admitted the truth instead of getting defensive, Nya looked at her with a mixture of love and compassion. "Oh, Sabrina. I know you want their acceptance, and I can't imagine how deeply that cuts you. But what if Mason's right? What if one of them is behind the broken window?"

"But what if they're not?"

"Well," Nya quickly said, "then the fact that the police questioned them as possible suspects should make them stop and reflect on how horribly they've treated you. It should make them ashamed of themselves, not angry with you. The truth is, you should be able to confidently rule them out as suspects but you can't. And after what Mason witnessed the night of your father's party, how can you blame him for being suspicious of them?"

Hearing it put so rationally, Sabrina couldn't refute Nya's words. She dropped her head down on the desk and groaned.

"You're right," she said after a moment. "I don't know why I overreacted. It's just…I didn't want them to have further ammunition to use against me."

"If they hold this against you, then I'd wipe my hands of them forever. And your father… You have carried way too much guilt where he's concerned already. I agree with Mason—he needs to man up and be a part of your life, no apologies."

Sabrina nodded, but her stomach was pulsing. "You're right. I can see that now. Gosh, I was so stupid. It's just when he talked to the cops about my father's family, he caught me off guard. Then suddenly I felt I had to put my guard back up."

"He was looking out for you, but you're too stubborn and self-sufficient to be able to accept a man stepping in to protect you."

Sabrina whimpered.

"And telling him to leave, when all he was trying to do was look out for you." Nya's expression was dumb-founded. "God knows you could handle a man taking care of you for a bit."

Sabrina bit her inner cheek. Nya was being a great sounding board, making her realize just how ridiculous she had been yesterday. But at the time, all she could remember was how her ex had tried to take control of so many aspects of her life and Sabrina had reacted instinctively.

Sabrina pressed the palms of her hands to her cheeks. She hadn't told Nya about the racy photo session, or how she had given Mason the SD card from the shoot. He must have seen that as the "Nice knowing you" kiss off. "What do I do?"

"Obviously, you call him. And apologize. And you tell him that you understand why he did what he did, and that you appreciate him looking out for you."

Sabrina wasn't sure she could tell him all of that—groveling wasn't her style—but she did plan to at least apologize. So she called, but Mason didn't answer. Instead, she sent him a text and told him that she had reacted badly the day before, and that she was sorry.

Then she waited.

And waited.

The arrival of the window repairman temporarily took Sabrina's mind off of Mason, but the moment he was gone, she went to check her phone. No reply.

The hours ticked by, and even after Sabrina completed two photo shoots, spoke with the photo lab about an error on a large print she was surprised—and hurt—that Mason didn't have anything to say in response to her text.

She knew she hadn't been nice to him, but was he that upset that he couldn't accept her apology?

Mason's lack of a response weighed on her mind for hours. Even worse, it weighed on her heart.

Well, I'm not going to grovel, she said to herself. *If he's so angry he can't—*

The sound of her cell phone interrupted Sabrina's thoughts, and she quickly snatched it up from her desk.

Got your message. I'm in Orange County helping to fight a forest fire. Have fun in New York.

Sabrina's elation over seeing Mason's text morphed into disappointment. He had responded, yes. But he hadn't said anything about her apology, which had left her feeling uncertain.

She sent him a return message, telling him to take care of himself. She hadn't realized that he had left town to go to work. However, she'd heard about the massive fire on the news and knew that it was spreading, so she wasn't surprised to learn that firefighters from other cities had gone to help out. She was worried about him. Firefighters died fighting forest fires, and he was immediately in harm's way.

She watched the clock, waiting for a reply from Mason. It didn't come.

But as the end of the work day rolled around, Sabrina had other concerns. Like packing everything she needed for New York.

"He's in Orange County, fighting a wildfire," Nya reminded her. "He's busy."

"I know," Sabrina conceded. Still, she wished he would reach out to her again.

"You really like him," Nya said, a sense of wonder in her voice. "Really, really like him."

Sighing softly, Sabrina turned from the newly replaced window where she'd been standing and faced Nya. "This is exactly why I hate dating. Things can be going so well, then suddenly you're unsure…I *hate* this feeling."

"It's part of the experience," Nya told her.

"Experience," Sabrina said and scoffed. "Like it's a theme park ride. *The experience of love. The highs, the lows. The thrills, the despair.*"

"Well, that sorta is what it is," Nya paused. "The day is going to come when you realize you can't control every aspect of life. And that sometimes, the biggest thrill is in letting go."

The very idea made Sabrina shudder. Sure, she knew

she couldn't control everything. But she could certainly control the anxiety she felt when it came to dating.

If Mason wasn't going to forgive her, she wasn't going to beg and make a fool of herself. She would count her losses, and move on.

But she knew that task would be easier said than done.

Sabrina's weekend in New York was plagued with thoughts of Mason. He'd reached out to her, mostly texts because he said he was extremely busy. The wildfires were still raging and he along with the other firefighters were working long, hard hours.

When Sabrina came back from New York, Mason was still out of town. On Monday, he said he anticipated returning on Tuesday. But when Tuesday rolled around, Mason told her that his date of would likely be Thursday.

"We're way busier here than we expected. This fire… it's a beast. But we finally turned the corner, and I'm coming home tomorrow," he'd told her.

A part of Sabrina was elated…but there was still a level of uncertainty between them. Their conversations that week had been mostly short, given Mason's long hours and fatigue level when he'd finished for the day. But there had been no real lovey-dovey talk. No *I miss yous*. Their brief phone conversations had been mostly about catching up. Even when Sabrina had had the chance to apologize to him again, there hadn't been much discussion afterward because Mason's phone had lost reception. In subsequent conversations, the topic had not been broached again.

"I'm glad you're safe," Sabrina said. "When I heard about two firefighters getting killed…" Her voice trailed off.

"You were worried about me?" Mason asked, and for the first time she heard a bit of playfulness in his voice.

"Of course," she said. "I don't want you to get hurt."

She paused. "You don't worry? I mean, when another firefighter gets killed at the very fire you're fighting…it doesn't scare you?"

"If I worried about getting hurt or killed, I couldn't do my job," Mason said. "Ask any firefighter. We all feel the same. We run into fires because that's what we're trained to do. We don't think about what could go wrong, only about how to stop the blaze."

"Wow," Sabrina said, truly in awe over that fact.

"By the way, watch the news later tonight," Mason said. "News crews were there when I saved a fawn. It's the kind of feel-good moment that will probably make the news."

"Oh, wow. I definitely will."

"Since I'm going to be back tomorrow," Mason began the tone of his voice lower now, "what are you doing this weekend?"

A slight frown marred Sabrina's face. She would love nothing more than to reconnect with Mason, but she had another out of town wedding.

"Actually, I'm out of town. I'm going to Mexico for a couple of days."

"Mexico?" Mason asked.

Sabrina almost regretted the timing of the trip. Having not seen Mason for over a week, she now craved him. "Another wedding. It's that time of year. The couple really loves me and my work, so they're paying to send me to Cancun for a couple of days to capture their special day."

"That's pretty special. Obviously, that speaks highly of your reputation. When exactly are you going?"

"Friday morning. I suspect you'll be back late tomorrow, which means I won't be able to see you."

"You said no to my offer of New York, but how would you feel about company in Mexico?"

The idea was certainly tempting. Time with Mason in Mexico? Who wouldn't enjoy that? But business came first for Sabrina, and it could be no other way. "It's a good thing I said no to you joining me in New York because I was run ragged. The couple even wanted late night shots on the hotel rooftop after the reception. So…as tempting as it is, when I'm paid to be a photographer on an out-of-town shoot, my time really belongs to the people who hire me."

"Okay, then when are you leaving?"

"Sunday."

"How about I meet you on Sunday, then? I can fly in then to make sure I'm not there on the couple's time. We'll have most of Sunday together, and we can stay till Monday or Tuesday. I'm sure I can get the time off after all these days in Orange County. Then you and I can enjoy the time in paradise as we see fit…"

His voice ended on a suggestive note, and Sabrina could imagine the smile on his face. The idea was absolutely tempting, but it was impossible. "I can't afford to extend my trip," she said.

"I'll pay for the expense."

"That's not what I mean," Sabrina said. "Seriously, it's a very tempting offer, but I have to be back here for Monday, anyway."

"Oh." Mason sounded disappointed. "What do you have planned for Monday?"

What did she have planned? "I've got work. Meetings with potential clients."

"For more weddings?"

"Yes. I have to go over package prices and options. Like I said, it's a busy time of year for me."

"Nya can do that, can't she? I'm sure she must know everything about your business."

"That's beside the point."

"Babe, I'm offering to fly to Mexico to spend time with you there. We haven't seen each other for a week. You, me, a Mexican hotel room for a couple of days? Surely you can miss a day of work for that…"

"I can't believe you'd even ask me that. I wouldn't ask you to blow off your career for me."

"Babe, it's a day. I thought you would want to see me."

"I do. But I wouldn't expect you to shirk your responsibilities for me."

"The nature of your job is different," Mason said, beginning to sound frustrated. "You're self-employed. That gives you some leeway. If you don't actually have any photo shoots scheduled for Monday, I don't see why—"

"Because I have a business to run. And if I skip work every time I feel like it—to roll around in the sand, no less—how will I grow my clientele? I've worked hard to build my business to what it is, and I'm not about to blow off my obligations. Same as you wouldn't."

"I'm not saying you should *blow off* your obligations. But having Nya handle some tasks I'm sure she's capable of—"

"Oh, so you know all about running a photo studio, do you?" Sabrina snapped.

"That's not what I said."

"I'm tired of people telling me how I should run my business."

"Telling you how to run your business?" Mason sounded dumbfounded. "You think that's what I'm doing?"

Sabrina's stomach tightened. "I— No, of course not."

"What am I? Your ex-husband?" he asked. "Is that what this argument is about?"

Sabrina blew out a frustrated breath. "I'm not saying that. I'm just trying to tell you that it's important for me to meet all of my business obligations, which includes more than doing the photo shoo—"

"Then do that," Mason told her. "I wasn't holding a gun to your head. Call me crazy, but I just thought you might have liked the idea of me heading to Mexico to spend time with you. Something different. Something spontaneous."

"And it would be."

"But you're not interested," Mason said. "I heard you loud and clear. That's my other line. I'll talk to you later."

A beat passed. Then Sabrina said, "Mason? Mason, are you there?"

But all she got was dead air in response.

He was gone.

Mason ended the call with Sabrina, then stood and tossed his smartphone onto the hotel bed. Groaning in frustration, he began to pace the room.

He was baffled. And disillusioned. Sabrina was actually blowing him off. When another woman would jump at his suggestion.

But not Sabrina who didn't need a man, much less want one it seemed.

Why was he even bothered by her rejection? After her reaction when he'd told the police about her family, he had started to wonder what they really had. A man should be able to take care of his woman, but the very idea seemed to anger Sabrina. Long-term, how could he be with her if she wouldn't open up her heart?

Women wanted romance, or so they claimed. Offering to pay to extend her plane ticket, plus get a hotel for two days of alone time qualified as romantic, didn't it?

Of course it did, and Mason knew there were other women who would definitely appreciate that kind of gesture.

Women like Kenya.

Only Kenya would drag him to all of the boutique shops and tell him that she liked this, and that, and she would rub against him and giggle. And he would end up spending a fortune buying her more status symbols to add to her collection.

Mason had expected the exact opposite of Sabrina, which was one of the reasons he wanted to go out on this limb and plan for a romantic two days. He wanted to do a big gesture that would put a smile on her face, especially since they hadn't been able to spend any time together lately.

"Why am I even bothering?" God knew, he'd never wanted anything serious with Sabrina. Or with any woman. He didn't do serious. When they'd first met, he'd felt the sparks between them and he had wanted her in his bed. It wasn't supposed to be more than that.

But somehow, it had become more than a fling.

Sabrina had come into his life, and he'd suddenly started thinking about having someone permanently in his life and growing old with them. He saw how miserable his father was being alone, pushing away any woman who could possibly love him despite his alcoholism.

No one wanted to die alone.

Except, perhaps, for Sabrina. As long as she had that camera of hers in her hands, she'd probably die a happy woman.

Chapter 19

Monday came and went without a call from Mason. This bothered Sabrina more than she realized.

She'd had a great weekend in Mexico, with the bride and groom. And their families had been thrilled with the work she had done. But on Sunday, when she'd had time to herself, she couldn't help but think about Mason's offer to join her at the resort. As she'd walked the grounds, relaxed on the beach and dined, she had seen happy couples all over the place.

And she'd been all the more reminded of how alone she was. Had she made a mistake by telling Mason no?

She knew she had reverted back to her arguments with her ex-husband. All she'd seen was that she was making one compromise for Mason, and she knew that one would lead to two, and two would lead to more. And of course, he would always expect her to be the one who made the compromises, because of course, his job was too important.

She had overreacted. Gone for anger instead of rationally explaining to Mason her fears. She knew she'd handled the situation badly.

To make matters worse, her morning appointment hadn't even shown—making it clear that she could have indulged in time with Mason in Mexico.

Once again, she sent Mason an "I'm sorry" text, and tried briefly to explain the reason for her reaction.

An hour later, when Nya came to deliver a message,

she was crestfallen. "Tom Sully called while you were in your meeting," Nya said. "He said he's back in charge of the firefighter calendar and wanted to schedule a time to meet with you."

Sabrina could hardly speak. Mason had stepped down? Her stomach sank. Obviously, she knew why. He didn't want to see her.

"Fine. I'll call him back."

"Okay, why are you so glum?" Nya asked her, sitting in the chair in front of her desk. "You went to Mexico, for goodness' sake. You should still be beaming."

Maybe if she'd had used a full day to have mind-blowing sex, she would be beaming. Not to mention, much more relaxed.

"Nya, I think I messed up," Sabrina said with a groan. "And this time for good."

Nya looked at her with concern. "What happened?"

Sabrina told her about Mason's offer to join her in Mexico.

"And you told him no?" Nya looked at her with a dumbfounded expression.

"I know, I know. It's just…if I start making all the concessions and put my job on the backburner, then what? I start losing all of my clients and my business goes downhill."

"You are truly starting to lose it. You know what the cure is for that? Twenty-four hours in bed with a hot guy in Mexico."

"I know…I screwed up."

"You're damn right you screwed up. For God's sake, just because Lester was a jerk about your career doesn't mean that every guy will be. Mason wanted to treat you to a fairytale most women only dream of…and you acted like he wanted to have you chained to a stove or something."

Sabrina groaned. "He…he hasn't responded to my text."

"Can you blame him? He tried to do something nice for you, and you rejected him. People can only take so much rejection."

Sabrina's heart began to pound hard. "You think he's never going to talk to me again?"

Nya shrugged. "I don't know. I do know that you can't sit around expecting him to be the one to call. You need to call him. Better yet, go see him. Tell him you messed up because you got scared. Whatever. Just tell him something that makes sense."

Sabrina bit down on her bottom lip for several seconds, contemplating Nya's words. And she decided that Nya was right. After calling the firehouse to determine that Mason was working, Sabrina first headed to Jean's Treats. She then made her way to the firehouse.

A bag of goodies in hand, Sabrina decided to walk to the firehouse. The walk would give her time to rehearse what she would say.

Her stomach tickled with nerves as she rounded the corner and the bay area of the firehouse came into view. She paused and inhaled a deep breath. Then, steeling her shoulders, she moved forward, determined to make Mason understand that she had been an idiot where he was concerned for the last time.

As she approached, she saw Mason standing just within the doorframe. His back was to her, and he was wearing his turnout pants and a navy-blue t-shirt. Her heart began to beat faster, but she forced a smile and continued to walk.

She slowed her pace when she realized that Mason was talking to someone. *A woman.* She watched with curiosity. Uncertain. But when the woman put her hand on Mason's shoulder and let it linger there, Sabrina's heart began to spasm.

The woman's hand went from Mason's shoulder and down his arm, in an undeniable caress.

Sabrina was stunned. Her heart began to accelerate as a queasy sensation filled her belly.

The woman must've sensed that someone was staring at her, because her gaze traveled in Sabrina's direction. They locked eyes.

The woman was gorgeous. Tall and thin with legs that went on for days. She was wearing a dress that highlighted her large cleavage. The type of dress meant to entice.

Sabrina's gaze flitted to Mason, who was now looking in her direction, as well. His lips parted, but he said nothing.

Quickly spinning around, Sabrina ran, dropping the bag of sweets in her haste to get away.

How could she have been so stupid? Obviously, Mason had already moved on. That was why she hadn't heard from him. There was a new woman in his life, a leggy, gorgeous one who looked like a supermodel. Exactly the type of woman a man like Mason would lust after.

Was he already sleeping with her?

Sabrina had spent days telling herself that she could walk away from Mason if she had to. But, the reality that he had moved on, hurt her deeply.

Lost in her thoughts as she approached her studio, she became startled after hearing a voice from behind shout her name.

Looking back in shock, Sabrina saw a woman wearing a huge smile and holding a microphone. She then noticed that a man with a video camera slung over his shoulder accompanied the woman. On the sidewalk in front of her shop was a white news van with Channel 2's logo painted across it.

"Yes," Sabrina said cautiously. "I'm Sabrina Crawford."

"I recognized you from the photos on your business cards," the woman said. "My name is Chelsea Williams, with Channel 2 news."

Sabrina took the woman's hand, and shook it. "Ah, yes. I've seen you on TV."

The woman continued to beam, as though her smile had been painted on. "Great. I'm here today to talk to you about the firefighter's calendar you're working on. And in particular, I would love to hear your thoughts about Mason Foley."

"Oh. What would you like me to tell you?"

"Well, for one thing, the city is certainly celebrating his heroics today. A couple of weeks ago, he saved a manager from a burning restaurant. And who wasn't touched by that photo of him carrying that baby deer from the wildfires. What was it like to work with a real, live hero?"

Sabrina looked over Chelsea's shoulder, to the cameraman. He was recording. Facing Chelsea again, she answered, "It was fine."

"Did he talk to you about his bravery?" Chelsea supplied.

"We talked about what drives him to want to save people."

Chelsea's eyes widened. "Wonderful. What did he tell you?"

Sabrina suddenly wasn't sure what she should say. It wasn't like what had happened to Mason's mother and brother was a secret. Certainly reporters would be able to dig into that history.

"He had a very personal situation where fire touched his life. And that's what drives him," she chose to offer instead.

"How was it working on the calendar with him?" Chelsea's eyebrows rose.

"He was a natural," Sabrina supplied.

"That's no surprise. Talk about sexy!" Chelsea fanned herself with her free hand. "What can the women of Ocean City expect to see when the calendar comes out?"

At first, Sabrina didn't understand the question. But she quickly caught on. "There are definitely some amazing shots of Mason that won't disappoint."

"With his shirt off?"

"With his shirt off."

"I can't wait." Chelsea's smile became a little mischievous. "Did he say whether or not he's single?"

Sabrina swallowed uncomfortably. Certainly these people had other things to report, she quickly though. But Chelsea Williams was staring at her expectantly, waiting for an answer.

"From what I understand, yes. He's single."

Chelsea then turned to the camera and said, "There you have it, ladies. Mason Foley, undeniable hero, is single. Be sure to check out the firefighter's calendar for the upcoming year, which should be available in October. I'm Chelsea Williams reporting for Channel 2 news."

Chelsea lowered the microphone and said, "Thank you for your time. I appreciate you sharing your thoughts."

Sabrina shrugged. "Sure."

"Mason Foley is certainly one hunk of a man. Lord knows I would love one hot night with him."

Sabrina's eyes widened as she looked at the reporter.

"Sorry. I know that wasn't professional. But hey, I'm still a woman. And Mason is definitely gorgeous. If he's single, I think I might just invite him out for a drink when I talk to him later."

"You're going to talk to him, too?"

"Mmm-hmm. I'm seeing him later at the fire station to discuss his heroics."

As Sabrina watched the woman scurry off, she felt a

tightening in her chest. Even Chelsea, a professional journalist, was going all gaga over Mason.

And Sabrina started to feel the same sense of uneasiness she'd felt when she'd first met him and he'd asked her out. Hadn't she vowed not to fall for that kind of guy? Mason's history of being a bachelor, and never being married at his age spoke volumes. No, it wasn't illegal or even immoral, but it was a cause for concern. It spoke of an inability to commit.

By the time she watched the six o'clock news, the uneasiness had turned into something else altogether— heartbreak. First up was the clip from her interview, where she looked much like a deer caught in the headlights. She almost seemed robotic as she spoke about the firefighter's calendar. Then came the clip with Mason.

Chelsea Williams unabashedly gushed over Mason as she spoke with him. But the blow to Sabrina's heart came when she asked him if he was single.

"Yes," Mason said with a charming smile. "I'm single."

The reporter's eyes had lit up, as though it was a personal invitation extended to her.

Chelsea had turned back to the camera saying, "You heard it, ladies. He's single! But be warned, ladies. I might just have to take a run at Mason Foley myself." Chelsea giggled like a school girl, leaving Sabrina wondering how someone like her had gotten the job she did. Clearly, she couldn't treat a story with the professionalism it deserved.

Scoffing, Sabrina turned the television off.

Yes, I'm single. The words played over and over again in her mind. If he was single, what on earth had they been doing for the past several weeks?

Sabrina swallowed painfully. She knew what they'd been doing. Sleeping together. And clearly, while her feelings had been deepening, Mason had clearly just been satisfying a need.

She went back downstairs to her studio and fired up her computer. Work would help keep her occupied, because continuing to think about Mason was going to make her nuts. She then found the folder with the photos from the wedding in Cancun and began to sort through them.

A solid hour passed as she diligently poured herself into her work. And suddenly, there was a loud crash. Her heart leaped into her throat, and prickles of fear spread through her body.

The front window had been broken again! She was sure of it.

Sitting still, she could barely breathe, not sure what to do. Mason had been with her the first time this had happened, but now she was alone. Worse, she couldn't help but feel that Mason was right. The first incident of violence couldn't have been an isolated event.

Was that the sound of movement? Her stomach lurched violently. Sabrina jumped up and ran to her office door, which she quickly closed and locked. Then she grabbed the chair from in front of her desk and jammed it beneath the doorknob for extra security. Hopefully, if someone had come into the building, they wouldn't be able to get through her office door.

Then she waited, listening quietly as the sound of her pulse thundered in her ears. She could hear something, but what? A sort of rustling sound?

Just as the fire alarm began to blare, Sabrina smelled the smoke.

Panic clawed at her throat. Smoke? Her studio on fire? Racing to her office door, she put her hand on the knob, and then jerked it back in pain. Then knob was so hot, it had burned her.

Looking around, a sense of desperation came over her. Her studio was windowless, providing no avenue of escape.

"What do I do? Oh, God. Help me!"

She had no choice. She had to get out of the office.

Her mind scrambling, she found a towel. She ran back to her door and used it to turn the knob. Sabrina began to feel a sense of relief as the door opened, but that relief dissipated as clouds of smoke and flames violently greeted her.

All the training she'd learned on how to escape a fire came back to her. Sabrina covered her mouth and nose with the towel and dropped to the ground. It was important to stay low.

Good God, how could the place already be engulfed? She held her breath for as long as she could as she tried to crawl toward the back door. The front of the store was lit up in flames, so there would be no escaping that way.

She took a deep breath, and began to cough. Her eyes were stinging. But with each second, she was closer to the exit.

She would make it.

Finally, she reached the door, and relief washed over her like the cold water she desperately craved. But when she came to her feet and tried to open the door, it wouldn't open.

Of course, the latches. Extra security to keep people from entering. Determined to get out alive, Sabrina felt for both of them and undid them. Then she turned the knob and pushed with all her might.

It still wouldn't open.

She shoved her shoulder into the door with every ounce of strength she had.

But it wouldn't budge.

"No!" Sabrina screamed, and tried again.

She rammed the door again and again with her left shoulder, until the pain was so bad she was sure she'd dislocated it. Tears filled her eyes and added to the burn of the smoke.

Why wouldn't it open? As Sabrina sank down onto the floor in defeat, the answer came to her.

The door was locked from the outside.

Someone had done this deliberately.

Someone had meant to kill her.

And they were going to get their wish.

Chapter 20

The alarm went off at the station. Mason and every other firefighter left the dinner they'd been preparing in the kitchen and immediately raced to the lower level.

"Engine Two, Ladder Two, Battalion Two," came the announcement over the loud speakers. "Structure fire at two-five-nine George Street."

Instantly, Mason's stomach filled with dread. Two-fifty-nine George Street?

Sabrina's studio!

He had tried to call her after she ran off, but she didn't answer her cell. And now there was a fire at her studio?

Like a well-oiled machine, the firefighters were in their respective trucks and on their way within a minute. Mason looked at Tyler, who was driving.

"Tyler, go as fast as you can. That's Sabrina's building!"

Tyler hit the sirens and the gas. No more than a minute and a half later, they were pulling up in front of Sabrina's studio. Mason saw the flames ripping through the front of the building, like a demon out to kill. The entire lower front structure was ablaze, and flames were now busting through a hole in the window at the front and clawing at the upper level.

As Tyler went to the water controls on the engine, Mason got a halligan tool and raced to the front of the store. He could see nothing inside, but began to call out to Sabrina nonetheless.

"Sabrina!" he wailed. "Sabrina, can you hear me?"

Her studio was in the back, and that's where Mason prayed she was.

He then charged around the side of the building.

"Captain Foley," someone called to him, but he didn't stop. He knew he wasn't supposed to enter the building alone, but if Sabrina was inside, he had to get to her.

"Stephenson, Duncan. There's a side door that leads to the upstairs unit," he said into his radio. "Check that. I'm going around the back to get into the lower level."

The first thing Mason noticed as he got to the back of the building was that her car was there.

The feelings of dread overpowered him. Sabrina was in the building.

"Stephenson, speak to me," he said into his radio. "Any sign of anyone inside?"

"It appears to be clear, sir."

Mason's eyes focused in on an object as he hustled to the back door. It was a piece of wood positioned from the door handle to the ground in order to jam the back door shut.

Mason grabbed at it, realizing it was far more taut than he'd expected. If Sabrina had been trying to escape this way, she wouldn't have had a chance.

He stomped on it, snapping the thick board. Then he quickly pulled on the door handle. Smoke billowed past him. Quickly, his eyes scanned the ground.

And that's when he saw her.

Crumpled on the ground.

Not moving.

"Sabrina!" Mason yelled, but she didn't respond.

He bent and quickly scooped her into his arms, tears stinging his eyes as he dismantled his respirator mask to put onto her face.

Her arms and legs were limp and he wasn't sure if she was breathing.

He ran faster than he ever had before with a victim in his arms toward the front on the property. "Medic!" he screamed as he headed straight for the paramedic vehicle.

The paramedics sprang into action, quickly grabbing the gurney off of the ambulance. One locked the wheels on it while the other got a stethoscope ready for use.

Mason placed Sabrina on the gurney and quickly stripped his gloves off of his hands. While the medic listened for a heartbeat, Mason frantically felt for a pulse.

"I don't feel a pulse!" he raged.

"I've got a pulse," the female paramedic said. "But it's weak. We've got to get her to the hospital. Let's move!"

Mason watched helplessly as the paramedics loaded Sabrina onto the ambulance and then affixed an oxygen mask from inside the vehicle to her face.

"She's the photographer, the one doing the firefighter calendar," Mason explained, barely able to speak.

"We know," the male said. "We'll take care of her."

Then the doors to the ambulance shut, and it took off, lights and sirens blaring.

Mason began to pray.

Pray that he hadn't forever lost the woman he'd fallen in love with.

Sabrina's eyes fluttered open. She didn't know where she was, only that her throat hurt. She inhaled and a sharp pain pierced her chest.

As her eyes came into focus, she blinked rapidly.

And then she saw Mason. Was she dreaming?

She blinked again. He was still there. His head bowed, his eyes closed.

But where was she?

"Mason?" she said, her voice croaking.

Instantly, his head shot up and his eyes opened. The anguish etched on his face was instantly replaced by overwhelming relief.

"Baby?" Tears filled his eyes and he reached for her hand. "Oh, God, you're awake."

Sabrina watched as he took her hand and placed it on his cheek. Emotions of pain and joy passed over his face. Turning his face into her hand, he kissed her palm, and then a shaky breath escaped his lips.

"Wh-where am I?" Sabrina asked. She tried to swallow, but her throat felt parched. "Wh-what happened?"

He shushed her. "Don't try to talk. Just…" His voice trailed off, and she could hear how it was ripe with agony.

"Where am I?" she pressed on.

"You're in the hospital," Mason explained.

She quickly jerked her head to the right, and saw the telltale signs of the hospital walls and heart monitor. She also realized that her right arm was attached to an IV.

Her eyes narrowed in confusion. Then the memory began to tickle her brain. Being in her studio. Hearing the loud crash. And then the fire.

"Oh, God," she gasped, feeling the same sense of panic she had when she'd been trapped in her studio. "It wasn't a dream."

"It's okay." Mason kissed her hand. "You're safe. You're fine. We got to you in time."

"I—I don't understand."

Mason stroked her forehead. "Save your strength. There'll be plenty of time to talk."

"The back door…it was locked." She spoke with difficulty, needing to get her words out. "I think…I think someone did this on purpose…"

"They did." Mason exhaled sharply. "The back door was jammed so you couldn't escape that way. A Molotov cocktail was thrown through your front window."

Hearing her theory confirmed, the panic continued to spread through her. "What?"

"You're very lucky to be alive." He kissed her hand again, his lips lingered on her skin. "I know you're afraid, but you're safe now. You did everything right. Covering your mouth, staying low. I will admit that you gave me the scare of my life. But you're going to be okay. And I'm not going to let anyone hurt you."

Sabrina glanced down and noticed that Mason was wearing his fire-resistant pants, with suspenders up over his navy-blue t-shirt. He had come straight to the hospital from the fire.

And then another thought came to her. "My—my mother. Father…"

"Are both aware that you're here," Mason supplied.

Sabrina frowned. What did that mean? "They're not here?"

"Sabrina, rest—"

Her breathing became labored. "Why is my family not here?"

"Baby, rest."

"I don't want to rest. I—I want to know—"

Mason placed a hand on her shoulder when she tried to sit up, forcing her to lie back. "They're here. But…they're downstairs." He paused. "With the police."

Sabrina's eyes narrowed. She didn't understand.

Mason held her gaze, and she could see that he was conflicted. Then he said, "The fire was arson, and the culprit's already been caught."

Sabrina's eyes widened in surprise. "What?"

"I was figuring I'd let your family tell you this, but they've been gone longer than I thought…"

"Tell me," Sabrina pleaded.

"Your father's wife," Mason began, and then stopped.

"She... Someone saw her smash your window. The guy followed her, held her until police came."

Though she felt queasy and weak, Sabrina sat upright. *"My father's wife? Marilyn?"*

Mason nodded. "Yes. Marilyn's actually here right now. She burned her hand when she started the fire, so she's being treated, as well. That's what your father's dealing with right now. And your mother. She had to be held back in fear she'd go after Marilyn. Both your parents were here to see you, but you were unconscious. Your half brother and sister, too."

Sabrina stared at Mason, not understanding.

"Your brother and sister feel awful about what happened, Sabrina. They're anxious to talk to you...which I anticipate will be soon. Once they're finished speaking with the police."

Sabrina's head swam, and it wasn't because she'd just survived a fire. What Mason had told her, she could hardly believe. From the news about Marilyn, to the reality that her siblings wanted to speak to her... It was all so overwhelming.

She squeezed Mason's hand as tears filled her eyes. Tears of relief and happiness.

"What is it?" he asked gently. "You want me to call the doctor?"

"No. I don't want you to leave me. Please don't go."

"It's okay," Mason told her. "I'm not going anywhere."

Closing her eyes, Sabrina fought to keep the tears at bay. She didn't succeed.

"Baby..."

Sabrina shook her head. She couldn't speak.

"You went through an ordeal," Mason said. "Being trapped in a fire. I know that was horrifying. But you're here. You're going to be fine."

He didn't understand. The memory of being trapped

in her studio wasn't what disturbed her at the moment. It was the fact that Mason was here, at her side, despite how she'd treated him.

She was about to tell him exactly how she felt when the door opened. Sabrina's gaze shifted in that direction. She saw her mother peering her head in, a worried expression over her face.

When Evelyn realized that Sabrina was awake, her eyes lit up with joy. She hurried over to Sabrina on the opposite side of the bed from where Mason sat.

"Oh, my baby!" She bent to hug Sabrina, and held her for a long time. "I was so worried."

Sabrina released Mason's hand to hug her back, and when her mother started to cry, Sabrina held her as tightly as she could. "It's okay, Mom. Don't cry."

Her mother pulled back, and a look of fury came over her face. "No, it's not okay. I could strangle Marilyn. In fact, I almost did. The police had to hold me back," she said almost proudly.

"I heard."

"At least she didn't get away unscathed. She has third degree burns to her hands. It's not like I wish her any pain. I know what I did years ago was wrong, but that woman needs to put it to rest and go on with her life. To take it out on you when it was never your fault…"

The night's events couldn't have come as a bigger shock to Sabrina, making one thing crystal clear. She had even more reason to feel bad where Mason was concerned. He was the one who'd suspected someone from her father's family, but she hadn't wanted to accept that. In fact, she'd let his belief cause friction in their relationship.

"I think maybe Marilyn was upset because I tried to reach out to Julia on Facebook," Sabrina guessed. "Maybe she felt threatened or something. But she shouldn't have.

Julia sent me back the nastiest letter. It's clear she wants nothing to do with me, either."

"I didn't write the letter."

At the sound of the voice, Sabrina and her mother turned their heads toward the door. Julia was standing there, Patrick close behind her. It was easy to see that they were siblings. Both from their resemblance, and also from the expression of disbelief and contriteness they both shared.

But what struck Sabrina most was the way she could see her own face in theirs, as well. They all resembled their father.

Julia took a tentative step into the room. "I told my mother about the note you'd sent me on Facebook, and was very upset. She didn't want me to respond to you, made me promise that I wouldn't. But...I wanted to. I wanted to start to get to know you, too."

"We're related," Patrick said. "That's the bottom line. And we should be a part of each other's lives."

Again, tears filled Sabrina's eyes. Was this really happening?

"We always stayed away because my mother hated the idea of us having anything to do with you," Julia explained. "And I'm sorry—I know at my dad's birthday celebration—our dad's birthday celebration—I wasn't exactly nice to you in the bathroom. But my mother was crying, and I believed...I believed her lies." Julia's face contorted with pain. "I'm so sorry. For everything."

Sabrina worked herself to a sitting position and extended both of her hands to them. Patrick and Julia came forward and took hold of her hands. "You're here now, that's what matters. And if you really want to get to know me—"

"We do," Julia insisted. "And not because of what happened. I've always wanted it. To think we could have lost you before we really had the chance to welcome you into our family…" Julia shook her head.

A smile spread on Sabrina's face as emotion filled her throat. "But that didn't happen. And today is the first day of the rest of our lives. That's what's important."

Julia hugged her hard, as though she never wanted to let go. Patrick wiped at his tears as Julia and Sabrina separated, and then he, too, hugged Sabrina.

"You're my sister," he said. "Not half. Just my sister. Same as Julia is."

Tears spilled from Sabrina's eyes at his words. This was all she'd ever wanted, to be accepted by the people who shared her DNA.

"You've got two nieces and a nephew to get to know, as soon as you're well," Patrick went on.

"Oh, wow." Sabrina wiped at her tears. A big family. She wouldn't have to feel alone anymore. "I can't wait."

"We couldn't be more sorry for what our mother did," Julia said.

"Maybe if we'd stood up to her when she had bad-mouthed you over the years," Patrick added.

"No, I was the one who should have stood up to her."

At the sound of her father's voice, Sabrina looked past her siblings to see her father walking into the room. Though she was smiling, new tears stung her eyes. "Daddy."

"I'm so sorry, baby," he said, approaching the bed. Patrick and Julia stepped back so that he could reach her bedside. "Her hatred ran too deep. I guess she never forgave me for what happened all those years ago." He looked over to Evelyn. "But I don't regret what I did. Not for a second. Because it gave me you."

Sabrina could no longer hold back her stream of tears. Never before had her father told her that he'd truly wanted her.

"Do you mean that?" she asked him, her voice sounding small.

A look of pain came over his face. "Of course." And then his voice cracked. "The fact that you even doubt that… I know I failed you as a father, and I'm sorry. But I will never fail you again. I promise you that. I love you, sweetheart. You're not a mistake. You were never a mistake." He glanced at Evelyn briefly before holding Sabrina's gaze again. "And you were conceived in love."

"Oh, daddy." Sabrina opened her arms wide to him, and he embraced her.

Finally, they parted, both of them dabbing at their eyes. Sabrina's eyes were going to be red and swollen after this, but she didn't care.

She had her family here. All of them.

"How is Marilyn?" Sabrina asked tentatively. "Was she hurt badly?"

"She'll live," her father said, anger causing his jaw to tighten. "But she'll go to jail, which is what she deserves. And I'll be consulting with a divorce attorney soon."

"I'm sorry," Sabrina said.

"I'm not," her father told her. "It's something I should have done a long time ago."

Sabrina's gaze shot upward when she saw Mason stand tall. "Where are you going?" she asked him.

"I figured I should give you some time with your family."

"No." And she extended her hand to him. "Come."

Mason stepped forward and took her hand. The sense of safety and security that came from his touch was profound. And she knew that he was the one who'd saved her.

"I know your unit was at the fire," she said, "but you're the one who saved me, aren't you?"

"Of course," he said simply, as if it could have been no other way.

He would protect her with his life. He would keep her safe. His love would lift her up, not knock her down. How had she ever doubted that?

She wanted to kiss him. Heck, she wanted to make love to him. But mostly, she needed to make him understand that she loved him.

"Will everyone please give me a moment alone with Mason? And wait a minute—where's Nya?"

"I didn't have a number for her," Mason said.

"Someone's going to have to call her," Sabrina said. "She's going to be livid if she hears about me being in the hospital on the news."

"Give me the number," Julia said. "I'll make the call."

Sabrina recited the number to her, and then her family left the room, leaving her alone with Mason. He pulled the chair he'd occupied closer to the bed and took a seat.

"What a night," Mason said. "Your brother and sister being here, and wanting a relationship with you. I know you must be elated."

"It's what I've always wanted. For my family to accept me, and become a part of my life."

"I'm happy for you."

"Mason," Sabrina said, and then sighed. "I'm so sorry. I treated you badly. I did my best to push you away, and it had nothing to do with you. And as much as I've always wanted my family's acceptance…if I got that tonight but lost you…" She closed her eyes pensively, emotion threatening to capture her again. "I would be devastated," she said through a cracked voice. "I know you might not believe that. And God only knows if you can find it in your heart to forgive me, or even to trust me… If you haven't already moved on. I was the biggest fool in the world, all because I was afraid. But—" She paused. "But please don't tell me it's too late."

The moments that passed seemed like hours as Sabrina waited for Mason's response.

Moments in which she didn't even breathe.

Then, finally, Mason lifted her hand to his lips and kissed it. "Do you know how I felt when I saw you out cold on your studio floor?" he asked. "I felt like my heart had been ripped out of my body. I've only ever felt devastation like that one other time in my life, when I lost my family in that fire. And the thought that I was about to lose the woman I loved to fire, as well? You can't begin to know the terror I felt as you were taken away in the ambulance. I wasn't sure if you would live or if you would…die."

Her eyes misted again, Sabrina put her second hand around Mason's, which were both clasped over her one hand.

"I love you, Sabrina. Almost from the beginning, I couldn't imagine my life without you. And that's the truth. I don't know why, but you came into my life…and into my heart. What you said to your brother and sister, about today being the first day of the rest of your lives, really struck me. Because that's the way I feel about us. That this is the first day of the rest of our lives. A life I want to spend loving and protecting you. If you'll let me."

For years, Sabrina had been searching for this feeling. This feeling of love and acceptance from her family…and from a man she could trust with her entire heart. "This is the happiest day of my life," Sabrina said, hot tears falling onto her cheeks. "The absolute best. I want you in my life. I want you to protect me, to love me. Maybe it took this happening to gain some clarity. But I know without a doubt that I can trust you with my heart. I love you, Mason. And for the first time in my life, I feel loved in return."

"You are, baby. You definitely are."

Sabrina angled her body toward his and framed his

cheek. "Then kiss me," she whispered. "Kiss me and never let me go."

A smile broke out on Mason's face. "Gladly."

He kissed her. The kind of kiss that reached into her soul and filled her with love.

The kind of love that she knew, without a doubt, would last a lifetime.

* * * * *

REQUEST YOUR FREE BOOKS!

2 FREE NOVELS PLUS 2 FREE GIFTS!

KIMANI ™ ROMANCE

Love's ultimate destination!

KROM13R